## *"Do you feel my dragon stroking you?*

"Close your eyes and listen closer," Nathan continued. "You will feel it."

Tracy did as he asked, trying to hear something other than the rapid beating of her heart. Suddenly she felt a presence inside her. An energy that throbbed and tingled deep in her core. Was that him rubbing against her womb? That's what it felt like—a thick, wonderful presence deep in her belly. Not physical, and yet she felt it so clearly.

And while she was focused so intently on the sensations in her belly, he bit the back of her neck. She gasped, arching in reaction. "Is that your dragon power?" She gasped again as the energy in her stomach shifted, seeming to slide up and down inside her. "Oh, God..."

Her entire body was trembling. It felt wonderful and terrifying at the same time. She had never even imagined sex like this.

"Don't think," he whispered. His mouth had dropped lower, tasting the skin just below the base of her neck. "Just feel."

And as she let herself go in his arms, she realized she didn't have any choice....

# Blaze™

Dear Reader,

I first discovered the Cult of the White Tigress at my favorite place in the world: a museum bookstore. What a find! Information on a group of women in China who raised sexuality beyond art into a religion. Women Tantrics. I could hardly believe it. And I certainly couldn't resist writing about them.

And what a great time I've had. I told my parents that this book explores issues of East meets West, sexuality as worship, and love as the answer to everyone's prayers. To my best friend, I confessed the truth: it was *fun!* I got to rediscover sexuality in a completely new way. After all, I had to study all those *other* research books, too. I even got to use a few concepts in my yoga class.

So now it's your turn. Open the book and see if you find something new. Then e-mail me at jade@jadeleeauthor.com and let me know what you think. Or visit me on the Web at www.jadeleeauthor.com.

Enjoy,

*Jade Lee*

# JADE LEE
## The Tao of Sex

HARLEQUIN®

TORONTO • NEW YORK • LONDON
AMSTERDAM • PARIS • SYDNEY • HAMBURG
STOCKHOLM • ATHENS • TOKYO • MILAN • MADRID
PRAGUE • WARSAW • BUDAPEST • AUCKLAND

ISBN-13: 978-0-373-79378-5
ISBN-10:  0-373-79378-2

THE TAO OF SEX

www.eHarlequin.com

**Printed in U.S.A.**

## ABOUT THE AUTHOR

Children of mixed races have their own set of rules. As the daughter of a Shanghai native and a staunch Indiana Hoosier, *USA TODAY* bestselling author Jade Lee struggled to find her own identity somewhere between America and China. Her search took her throughout Asia and the United States. In the end, the answer was found in writing fiction and the amazing power of love.

My heartfelt thanks to Brenda Chin for shaping this book beyond my best into fabulous.

Special kudos go to Pattie Steele-Perkins for making it all happen.

And to any living tigresses today, bless you and thank you for the inspiration.

# *1*

---

"WHY ARE YOU SO ANXIOUS to sell?"

Tracy Williams looked away from her Realtor to the apartment building that had been her life for the last eight years. She'd overhauled the plumbing, fixed the electrical, even wired for Wi-Fi. But it wasn't her future, not by a long shot. "I took over the building when my parents died," she said. "But now my brother's about to go to college and I've got to pay for tuition. Besides, it's time for me to move on. You know, find my life."

Mr. Curtis blinked, then continued to make notes on his pad of paper. Apparently, he wasn't one for chitchat. That was fine with her, she thought as she glanced at her watch. Ten minutes. 4C was due back from class in ten minutes, and she didn't want to be standing here with a man old enough to be her father when *he* returned. She wanted to be casual, open to conversation, even a little flirty—as she had been for the last month on Tuesdays and Thursdays at 3:15.

"When do you think you can find a buyer?" she asked while her gaze drifted to the front door. She loved that first moment when 4C rounded the corner. The afternoon sun would glint in his gorgeous dark eyes, and he was often frowning in concentration. The wind played with his silky black hair just like in a movie, and she would get light-headed from the absolute potential of the moment. Anything could happen. She could be light and funny, or mysteriously sensual. She could say something brilliant that would lead to more. Maybe one day she'd have the kind of night she fantasized about but never acted on because she was acting as a single mom to her teenage brother.

Or she could stand here like an idiot while her Realtor made notes. "Do you think it will be enough to pay for two sets of college tuition? For me and my brother?"

"Hard to say," he answered, his nose still in his notebook. "You know the basics—keep the place clean, the plumbing flowing, the tenants happy." He looked up, his gaze unwaveringly cold. "The little things matter, Miss Williams. A little dirt can cost in the overall impression and that affects the price." He narrowed his eyes at her. "Do you think you can do that?"

She lifted her chin. Eight years ago, she'd known nothing about apartment buildings or about raising her preteen brother. Being a landlord had been her father's dream, not hers. One awful car accident later, and this building was her and her brother's only means of support. Thankfully, it had been enough. Now, Joey was a solid B student with a bright future, the building had been renovated within an inch of its life, and she had already downloaded her applications to the best business schools in the nation. "I can do it," she said firmly.

"See that you do." Then he snapped his leather folder shut, spun on his heel and left, nearly running over 4C at the front door and ruining her favorite moment of the day. Tracy barely managed a gulp before she stood face-to-face with her fantasy man: Mr. Nathan Gao of Hong Kong, currently an MBA student at the prestigious University of Illinois, and walking Chinese sex god. He wore a summer suit too cold for October and carried a battered leather attaché case gripped in elegantly long fingers whitened with cold. His hair was cut conservatively—black silk that tended to fall raggedly about his eyes. His skin's golden color seemed rugged with his hint of a beard. And his eyebrows were like dark strokes of a fine ink brush. How pathetic was that? She thought his eyebrows were sexy. His shoulders were hunched against the wind, but that only gave him a sweet rumpled appearance, especially since they were broad enough to appear strong even curled against the cold. With no apparent effort at all, he swerved to avoid Mr. Curtis then hauled the doors open despite the wind. Then he looked up and smiled.

That smile had lived in her dreams. His mouth was pale but still sensuous, full in ways she hadn't expected from a Chinese man. It was sexy enough when he was serious, but his smile sent shivers down her spine, especially when it was aimed straight at her. God, what things he had done to her with those lips! Fantasy lovers were the best.

She slammed her mouth shut and tried not to look like a lovesick teen. Just because she'd lived as a monk for the last eight years didn't mean she had to act like an adolescent. She was an adult, a suave woman. One who had just sucked in her stomach when her fantasy man turned and smiled at not one, not two, but four giggling college girls. Crop tops and blond ponytails bobbed in the wind as they entered the building. They were chattering a mile a minute, giggling and flirting for all they were worth—which from the looks of their jewelry was quite a lot. And even worse, Nathan Gao was flirting back. His head was dipped in shy modesty while a blush stained his cheeks. Then he gestured up the staircase.

"My studio is on the fourth floor, ladies."

"Why don't you lead the way?" chirped the one brunette.

Mr. Gao nodded, then started climbing while everyone in the hall—Tracy included—ogled his perfect behind.

Tracy's shoulders tightened with irritation as the blondes nearly ran her over. They hadn't even realized she was standing there! By the time the brunette came close, Tracy had a plan. All four girls carried flyers on bright red paper. An ad of some sort and obviously related to their presence here.

"May I?" she asked as she slid the flyer out of the brunette's hand.

The girl blinked and dimpled prettily. "Sorry, ma'am, but I'll be late for class." Then she sprang up the stairs like a cheerleader.

Tracy felt a gut punch from being called *ma'am.* Sure, her navy blue business suit made her look older, but not *that* much older. Unable to deal with the thought, she read the flyer.

*TANTRIC SEX CLASSES*
*Learn the secrets of SEXUAL IMMORTALITY*
*Experienced Dragon Master*
*Group, couple or individual*
*Privacy Guaranteed*
*$10 a class*
*Contact Nathan Gao*

Tracy read and reread the flyer. Sex classes? In her building? *Sex classes!* She frowned, trying to sort through the possibilities. This was a college campus with all sorts of unusual classes. His could be nothing more than what it proclaimed—classes in an exotic religion.

She snorted. She didn't have that kind of luck. Besides, it didn't matter. The cops and the university were on an aggressive clean-up-campus campaign. They liked splashy, front-page arrests even if the charges were dismissed later. "Sex Classes" would be prime targets for their arrest-first, ask-questions-later tactics.

She looked out the door to where Mr. Curtis was just now pulling out of the parking lot. If a little mud in the hallway made a bad impression, what would a vice bust do? Whether or not 4C was actually doing something illegal wouldn't matter. It would still be front-page news at exactly the wrong time. And if she lost her status as "University Approved Housing" because of a splashy vice bust, then Tracy's entire future was sunk. Without approved status, the value of the building tanked. Once the value tanked, no way would its sale cover two sets of college tuition. 4C's Tantric class could derail her entire future.

She crumpled the flyer in her fist as she mounted the stairs, her footfalls growing heavier and harder with each step. She hit the landing at full speed then fumbled trying to get out her master key. Normally it was in her back pocket, but today she wore the damn suit that apparently made her look like Grandma Moses. She had to search for it in the bottom of her blue plastic binder while listening to giggles that carried easily through the door.

Got it! Pulling out the key, she slipped it silently in the lock. She'd already developed a plan. She would gasp in horrified shock at whatever they were doing—the giggles were getting even louder—then calmly demand that Mr.

Nathan Gao vacate immediately. That was the best solution. She'd refund his money, even help him move. "No harm, no foul," she'd say. "Just go teach your 'classes' on someone else's property." It was a blow to her fantasy life, of course. She'd have to wait even longer to open the door to her sexuality, but when had anything ever gone how she'd planned?

She pushed open the door, her gasp already begun. Only to have her breath choked off in real shock. Mr. Gao was almost naked. Gone was his shirt, jacket and shoes. He was kneeling on the floor, his chest totally bare, as he addressed the equally topless coeds. Mr. Gao looked up, his sculpted black eyebrows raising in a silent question. But Tracy couldn't form any words—righteously indignant or not. Her mind—and her eyes—were completely trained on Mr. Better-Than-Jet-Li. She'd been dreaming of having that chest over her, beneath her, beside her, but she'd never guessed how really ripped he was. His skin was light gold in the afternoon sun, his shoulders pulled back in perfect posture that absolutely accented his six pack—no, *twelve*-pack—abs. No fat softened the lean beauty of his torso and when he slowly stood, Tracy could do no more than stare open-mouthed at him.

"Mrs. Williams, what is the meaning of this intrusion?"

His voice quivered down her spine and she had to forcibly drag her gaze up from the bare flesh just below his belly button. How often had she fantasized about tugging off his loose pants? How hideous was it that she finally got to see his fabulous body but in this context? She swallowed, but still couldn't pull her eyes off his sculpted abs.

"Ms. Williams," she murmured. "I'm not married." And what the hell did that have to do with anything?

"So sorry," he returned, his tone softening into that low bedroom voice she'd been imagining for months. "Are you here to join the class?"

Class? She blinked. Oh, that class! The possibly illegal sex class that was jeopardizing her entire future. She straightened, forcibly cooled her expression, and even managed a disdainful lift to her eyebrow. "I'm sorry, Mr. Gao, but I am not interested in your *class*. In fact, I am afraid I am going to have to evict you for illegal activity." She winced at the lie. He certainly wasn't doing anything illegal at the moment. But she wanted to come on overly strong so that she had room to compromise. "Please vacate the premises by tomorrow morning."

He reared back in shock, his chest muscles rippling in a truly stunning display. "Sorry? Illegal activity? It must be my English—I don't understand."

Yeah, right. His English was flawless. "Please. You can't think I'm that stupid." She canted her gaze—reluctantly—at the gaggle of girls who had miraculously pulled their cropped T-shirts back on. "I can't afford even the appearance of something unwholesome." Another wince. She sounded like a stuck-up prude. Time to offer up the compromise. "Please, just move out and I won't call the cops."

His entire body went rigid with indignation. "Unwholesome? Who's unwholesome?" He stared accusingly at the girls. As one, they gasped, then grabbed their designer purses and embroidered book bags. Three of the four made it out the door in a split second, but the fourth lingered.

"We didn't hire him for that," the petite blonde number one murmured. "This *was* just a class."

"Don't be naive," Tracy returned as the girl slipped past.

"Don't be a close-minded bigot!" Mr. Gao snapped.

Tracy felt her shoulders tighten. Fantasy lovers should never, ever become real. They were always a disappointment. "Just go, Mr. Gao. I can't take the risk of having you here," she said with real regret. "I just can't risk it. I'm sorry." She turned to leave, but he moved faster than she thought possible. Before she completed her pivot, he slipped in front of the door, blocking it with all that rippling muscle. He never touched her, but Lord, the sight alone was enough to stop her cold.

"I was teaching a class!" He spoke with barely repressed rage. He grabbed his flyer—the very same one she had still clenched in her fist—and pushed it toward her. "Tantric class. It's a religion."

She tilted her head back, startled—and a little intimidated—by his height. They'd never been this close before, and the heat off his body made her head spin. "It's a cover," she managed to say. "A convenient lie, and we both know it."

His eyes were flat and cold. "I know nothing of the kind, Miss Williams. I will not leave my apartment. You may call the police if you wish. I have done nothing wrong." Then his lips tightened in apparent disappointment. It was a small movement, but she was so close that she saw every nuance. "Come to a class," he urged. "Tantrism is just a belief system." He paused a moment, his eyes going flinty dark. "Unusual but completely legal."

"I can have you evicted," she bluffed.

"No, you can't. Imagine the problems, especially if I call the Chinese embassy."

She swallowed. A messy international argument involving religion would screw up the sale of the building almost as much as a vice bust. "You can't sell sex in the United States. It's illegal."

"Selling sex is one-hundred-percent legal as long as it is attached to a product. Having sex for money is illegal, and no one here was having sex."

"You're almost naked! They were topless." Her emotions were spiraling out of control, but she couldn't seem to stop herself. She had dreamed of this man for almost two months now, the last thing she wanted was to kick him out. But she couldn't risk her or her brother's future on anything that appeared immoral. "I'll refund your security deposit. I'll help you move. We can use my truck, but you've got to go. I'm sorry."

"I am not leaving." His voice was hard and flat—so different from the warm, flirty exchanges they'd been having since the beginning of school. Then he grabbed her by the waist and lifted her out of his apartment. She barely had time to squeak in alarm before her sedate black pumps touched gently down on the hallway carpet. "Excuse me while I call my lawyer," he said. Then he flashed his cell phone at her just before shutting the door firmly in her face.

Tracy glared at the thin door. She could force her way in there, but no way was she going to win against him in a physical fight. Not that it wouldn't be fun trying, but...

She pulled her thoughts back from the gutter and turned away, making sure she was noisy as she stomped down the hallway. Let the gorgeous hunk think he'd defeated her. As soon as she was out of earshot, she whipped out her cell phone and dialed, punching in the extension when prompted.

"Detective McKay."

She smiled. Thank God for old friends with helpful professions. "Hey, Mike. It's Tracy. Can you run a check for me on a tenant?"

NATHAN SNAPPED HIS cell phone shut. He didn't have any minutes left on his phone anyway, much less enough to consult a lawyer. It had taken all his money to get to the United States to study business at a prestigious school. An MBA from the University of Illinois would get him a first-class job with first-class pay. That money would in turn pay for his siblings' education and set them all on the right path. It was a weighty responsibility, but one he cherished as the eldest male of his generation.

How infuriating to have all that threatened by one close-minded American woman! He dropped his head against the door and cursed himself for a blind fool. He had noticed Ms. Tracy Williams, of course. She had stood out in his mind even before she'd become his landlord. Sweet, refreshingly nervous as a woman, but amazingly capable as a landlord, she had fascinated him from the first moment he'd visited her apartment building. Over the past two months, he'd seen her work on the roof in sweltering heat, muscle in a stubborn water heater, even crawl beneath the building as she rewired the cable, and yet when she spoke to him, she acted like a shy teenager. Her remarks were always casually fun, but her body language had sizzled with sensuality. It drew him, and he constantly wondered why she suppressed such natural sexuality.

Well, he had his answer now, didn't he? She was a prude. Damn the waste! Damn her for not even giving him a chance to explain. And damn her for still occupying his fantasies when the reality was so disappointing. Wow, had she looked hot in that blue business suit!

Pushing away from the door, Nathan mentally tabulated his bills. Forget food and rent, he had to pay for his education. With his fellowship abruptly disappearing three weeks ago because of government cutbacks, he needed to find a new job. But his student visa excluded everything else.

So he'd done the only thing he could: he'd begun teaching Tantrism. All he had to do was dress in tight pants and a muscle T-shirt, both borrowed from his neighbor, and post flyers at the nearby sororities. He knew they weren't interested in the true meaning of Tantric Buddhism—he was really selling a few hours of being ogled by rich American girls—but he was desperate. And if he could impart a few morsels of Truth while feeding himself, then so be it.

But not if Tracy Williams evicted him. Up until now, she hadn't seemed uptight, only innocent. As if she'd never been allowed to explore her sexual nature. He frowned. Something else was at work here. Something else was forcing her hand, but what? And how could he get her to change her mind?

He pictured Miss Williams in his thoughts. She had the curvy build of many Caucasians—lush bottom, tiny waist and full breasts beneath her tapered white blouse. Her face was just long enough, her complexion clear—milky-white, in fact—and her eyes were a bright brown. In truth, fortune sat on her face, lengthening her earlobes and sweetening the distance between the tip of her nose and the curve of her pale lips. He sensed a clarity in her chi—her energy—though like her body, it was buried beneath ill-fitting clutter.

It would be a joy to peel back the clothing on her body and the layers of grime on her energy. What a beauty would lie underneath. His own energy was already strengthening at the thought. It could be amazing for both of them, if she just allowed it. But first, he had to get close enough to show her the truth.

Fortunately, he had an idea….

# 2

"Urng ealtrr called."

Tracy looked up from her breakfast of champions—black coffee and plain yogurt—to frown at her younger brother. "What?"

Joey was trying to bulk for football, which meant he was eating everything in sight. Right now he was alternating between a three-egg omelet and a bowl of sugar-frosted something. He swallowed, slurped the last of the orange juice, then finally spoke clearly. "The Realtor called."

Tracy set down her coffee, a shiver of excitement zinging through her body. "Has he got an offer already?"

Joey stared at her, his sweet brown eyes completely flat. "No offer," he mumbled as he turned back to the omelet. "Just wanted details about when we inherited, how much debt was on the property, and how we leveraged it. Plus tax stuff and the dates of your renovations."

Tracy groaned. Great, more paperwork. "You told him to call my cell, right?"

"Nah. I answered it all for him."

It was a good thing Tracy had set down her coffee because it would have sloshed to the floor. "When did you pay attention to words like *leverage* and *taxes?*"

Joey set down his fork. "I haven't been asleep all these years. I know stuff."

"I'm sure you do," she said softly, more than a little thrown. Her brother wasn't stupid—but when had he noticed *anything* beyond football and the season's newest cheerleaders.

"I can help with the drywall this weekend, if you want," he said as he drained his cereal bowl with a loud slurp.

"Already done. Besides, don't you have a history paper to write?"

"Already done," he retorted. "Mandy helped me."

"Good. Then you can study for the ACTs. It's your last shot at a decent score—"

"I know!" Joey dropped his empty bowl on the table, his tone surly as only a teen could be. "God, you're really jonesing for it, aren't you? Four more years of school. Ugh!"

"Think of the money you can earn with an education." She leaned forward. "Joey, do you know how much a stockbroker makes in a year? One who's willing to work hard?" She sighed wistfully. "We'd never have to worry about money again."

"I'm not worried now," he returned. His long lashes dropped against his freckled face. He was still so young, and yet she saw adulthood in his broad shoulders and his quiet strength. He'd grown so much since that awful day eight years ago.

"*I'm* worried, Joey," she confessed. "Slow and steady, remember? That's what Dad used to say. Effort now is like putting pennies in a jar. Eventually it'll pay off."

He stacked his dishes and dropped them in the sink behind him. "I *have* been working hard."

She nodded. He'd certainly been working *out* hard.

Football was his passion, and he did all sorts of renovation work with her or for his friends' parents on the weekends. But that wasn't the same as working hard at school. "Joey, we're at the big payoff. After eight years, we can finally start living the lives we were meant to before…" She shrugged. "You know, before."

His gaze slanted away. He never liked talking about their parents. Truthfully, she didn't, either; it hurt too much. "I never asked you to give up your life for me," he said. "You could have gone to college. I would have found a way to get by."

She stepped forward, wanting to hug him the way they had so long ago. But he bunched his shoulders and leaned under the table to grab his backpack. So she tucked her hands tightly to her chest. "I wouldn't change a thing, Joey. These last years have been hard, yes, but they've been good, too. Come on, aren't you ready to move on? Go to college? Get started on adulthood?"

He straightened slowly, then faced her with a look that was half wary, half hopeful. "What if I took a year off? We have enough money for you to go to school, right? I could take care of the apartment building—"

"Absolutely not. You're going to college." He wasn't going to put his life on hold for her. "It's what Mom and Dad wanted."

His lips tightened. He never argued when she played the Mom-and-Dad card. "Why don't you ever date?"

She blinked, thrown for the second time this morning. "When did you start paying attention to my dating habits?"

"Mandy noticed. She said you ought to date more. That maybe you'd be less worried about money and stuff if you got out more." Translation: if she dated, she'd be less focused on him going to college.

"Nice try, but Mandy's wrong," she said. "The men I meet are all flash. None of them are in for the long haul. Besides, I'm working on me." She smiled, finally seeing a point to this conversation. "Yes, Joey, I am jonesing for it. It's time for us both to step into our adult lives. I'm willing to work hard for that. How about you?"

"Fine," he snapped as he pushed away from the kitchen table. "I'll try for a football scholarship."

"You'll try to ace that physics test on Monday."

He groaned as he shrugged on his backpack. "You know I'm not good at school."

"Don't make me be a mom here," she said in her most momlike voice. "Study for that test! Both of them!"

"Fine." He shrugged on the varsity jacket that had cost her $150 last Christmas. She'd skipped lunch for months just to save up for it. "Joey, just think about what we could have—"

"I'll study with Tommy after practice," he interrupted.

What could she say to that except a tired old adage? "Slow and steady effort, Joey."

He hauled open the back door. "I really liked doing the drywall and plumbing and stuff with Dad. With you, too." He paused long enough for Tracy to realize there was an underlying message there, but then he spun away and the screen door bounced shut behind him. She shifted sideways to watch out the window as he trudged to the bus stop.

How she wished she understood her brother. Some days he seemed so mature, happy with football, focused on being a high-school senior. Then the next moment, he seemed lost, looking to her to provide an answer when she didn't even know the question. What did he need? What was missing in his life?

She didn't know, and so she had no choice but to move on with her day. Painting and mopping were on the schedule. Wow. The glamorous life of a landlord. She flashed briefly on tenant 4C. Would he know what was going on with her brother? Did his Tantric religion offer answers to teenage boys, as well as sexual immortality?

Of course not. But the idea had her smiling all the way to the paint store.

WITH ONE FOOT, Tracy stomped on the mop-bucket squeezer. The water drained with a loud splash, then with a practiced whip slap, she obliterated more mud from the hallway. She'd finished painting in record time, and so now she had to do her bit as janitor. Her ancient Discman belted out her favorite mopping music, but nothing lifted her black mood this blustery day.

Then she accidentally swiped across a pair of knock-off Nikes—attached to one tall Chinese tenant—and her heart abruptly started beating pitter-pat. Then she remembered his Tantric class, and her mood darkened in annoyance—at him, at herself, at the whole situation that made the only interesting man she knew a financial risk she couldn't afford.

"Ah, hell," she muttered, unsure what she was cursing.

"No worries, Miss Williams," he said, his smile bringing his Asian charm to the fore. "My clothing has suffered far worse." His eyes sparkled with part shyness, part devilry, and once again she was reminded why he'd become the object of her fantasies. Everything about him begged her to look deeper. What mysteries lay just beneath his very intriguing exterior?

She yanked down her headphones. "I didn't see you there." She bit her lip then and tried not to get lost in his eyes. This was how it always went with him, even when she was prepared. He smiled and she lost all sense of who she was and what she wanted. Most days she simply smiled back. Occasionally she remembered rehearsed speeches. He was always polite, but she never got beyond the shock of wanting to be perfect for him, of feeling completely blindsided by his beauty even when she wasn't.

Today was no different except that this time her business side kicked in. Instead of little girl Tracy getting lost in his smile, businesswoman Tracy remembered that she had to sell this building. In eleven months, she needed two sets of tuition. So until Mike told her 4C did *not* have a criminal record, she couldn't risk being friendly with him. Or making any promises about letting him stay.

"I can't let you stay here. Not if you're teaching those classes."

His face dropped and she abruptly noticed that he looked tired. His skin was less golden, more wan. Backlit as he was by the afternoon sun, she could see that his shoulders were stooped and his head tilted slightly forward.

"I have to teach those classes," he said. "I cannot survive any other way."

She shook her head. "You can't. I'll have to evict you." She bit her lip. "Please don't make me do that."

Instead of answering, he started rooting through his scarred satchel. "I have something for you." He pulled out a couple of pristine white pages. "It's a list of tasks and their market value," he explained. "The Asian Student Group lists you as a landlord who exchanges work for a lowered rent, but I couldn't find a table of jobs. I thought if you had one, then you would get more tenants willing to upgrade their units. It also helps prevent arguments about the value of someone's work."

She began flipping through the pages and saw an impressive chart listing a whole slew of apartment upgrades starting with painting all the way through to furniture repair. "What," she quipped, "no plumbing or electrical work?"

He shrugged. "I didn't have enough time. But I could get you something by tomorrow if you like."

She stared at him, unaccountable fury building inside her. It was wrong of her—completely and utterly unfair to him. He was being nice. She wasn't really mad at him, it was more the whole situation: that she had to threaten a man she'd been fantasizing about for months. And yet, she couldn't manage to say that. "You don't get it, do you? I can't have you doing anything illegal here. Nothing that even appears illegal! Nothing that suggests anything illegal!"

She tried to shove the beautifully done pages back at him, but he didn't move. He simply stared at her with an open, startled expression. "You are angry," he finally said. "You are never angry."

She swallowed, not knowing what to say. "You aren't listening," she began, but he interrupted her.

"What is happening?" He took a step forward. "What is the real problem?" As he spoke, she felt as if his whole body opened to her, as if he really wanted to know. The sight was so unusual and so needed that she actually lost her breath. God, how she had dreamed of him asking such a question of her. And in her fantasies, she blurted it all out—her financial fears, her brother's weird moods, her dreams for the future that had been put on hold since that awful day eight years ago. But that was a dream, and this was reality.

There was no way his sympathy was real. They hadn't progressed beyond simple, awkward flirting before she'd tried to evict him. So she shut her mouth and closed her eyes, reminding herself over and over that everything he offered was fake.

"Thank you for the charts," she ground out as she shoved them into her back pants pocket. It was too small, so they teetered ridiculously back there, but she refused to fix it. Instead, she dared look him in the eyes again. "Quit teaching those classes." Then she grabbed the mop handle and prepared to wield it with a criminal vengeance.

"I can help you," he returned in a soft tone.

Shock made her rear her head back up. What was he talking about, helping her? It couldn't be with her worries. He didn't know anything about them. Did he mean the mopping? Or with something else? She didn't know how to respond except to gape at him. And damn if he didn't arch a really sexy brow at her that made her think of hot, sweet sex on a cold October day.

"Your chi is chaotic," he said, as if that explained anything. "Your energy is messed up. I can quiet it. It will make you think more clearly." He sighed. "Just take my hands. You don't have to believe."

He extended his hands—palms up—and waited. She felt no demand in his posture, just a simple offer of help with her chi. Whatever that was. If this was a come-on, it was the strangest one she'd ever experienced, and that alone won him points. Her curiosity was piqued. And she really did feel bad about treating him so rudely. So in the end, she took hold of his hands.

Nothing happened. Well, nothing except an abrupt realization that his hands weren't cold. Given that the hallway was pretty nippy that was startling enough. But his warmth was a delicious kind of warmth, like rich hot chocolate or a snuggling puppy wrapped in a heated towel. She tried to snort in disdain. Hot cocoa and a puppy? What was she? Twelve years old? And yet…

His heat was seductive. It enveloped her hands and tingled up her wrists. No, it wasn't a tingle, she realized, but a pervasive invasion of *yumminess*. Her gaze leaped to his, and her breath caught. His eyes were fixed on her face, but not such that he seemed to see her. Instead, he was looking through her or inside her or she didn't know where, but it was intense. Powerfully direct—like an arrow aimed straight at her heart—and yet silent and steady. If he was an arrow, he was flying clean and true straight at her.

She had the sudden urge to duck and cover, but it was too late. She couldn't move without breaking his wondrous heat. She couldn't even blink, so fascinating was his expression. A deer in headlights, that was what she was. A dumb animal too stupid to pull away. And yet, it felt so…

Angry. Infuriating. Boiling fear and frustration and hatred steamed off her skin. She felt her hands clench around his larger ones. Rage flashed through her body, exploding in the air between them…and was gone. *Poof.* As if it had been lifted right off her skin. The anger was gone, and she was left feeling…what?

Lost and inadequate. She didn't know how to help her brother, wasn't sure she could get into college much less make it once there, and most of all, didn't know if she could keep things together long enough to start a life that had been on hold for eight years. Everything was about to change, and she wasn't sure she could handle any of it.

"I'm not angry anymore," she said, awe infusing her

voice. In truth, she'd never really been angry, just overwhelmed. "My brother, Joey," she blurted. "I don't understand him. He seems to be reaching out, but I don't know what to do. I hate feeling so useless."

She refocused on his face, reality intruding with a sudden shock. What was she doing confessing that kind of personal detail to this man? Whipping her hands out of his, she took an unsteady step backward. "What did you do?"

His hands fell to his sides, but his expression remained calm, and his eyes begged her to touch him again, to feel that yumminess once again. "It is what I teach," he said softly. "Chi—personal energy—and how to purify it."

"What?"

He straightened, and his eyes grew softer and warmer. They were mesmerizing as he spoke, tempting her to believe anything he said.

"Every living thing has an energy field," he said. "We call it *chi*. The clearer your energy is, the clearer your thoughts are. I quieted your chi so you could think more clearly." He smiled. "That is what I teach. I show people how to clear their energy field."

She blinked, her mind whirling in confusion. "But the girls… I saw them. And you, too. You were all stripping!" She was babbling, but she couldn't seem to stop.

"Your chi is growing chaotic again." He extended his hands, but she backed away.

"Don't touch me!" Tracy didn't know why she was so vehement, especially since she *did* want to take his hands. She wanted to feel that incredible warmth sliding through her system again. She wanted *him,* and that thought terrified her more than all that other stuff about energy and chi and naked college girls. She felt confused and inadequate, which made him an even stronger temptation. She wanted to curl into his strength and lay all her fears at his feet. But she could not, not, not do that with this man! Not until she knew who he was and what he did. And yet, the desire was so strong.

She watched him bend down for his attaché case again. His expression was open, his body language charming, and his tush was really, *really* nicely formed. "I know it's a lot to handle, right now," he said. "But I have another class this evening at seven. Please come. Bring the police if you must, but come and see that what I teach is not illegal. It's not even immoral."

She wanted to shake her head. She wanted to say there was no way in hell that she would be sucked under his spell, but her mouth remained resolutely shut. Meanwhile, his hair was slipping across his forehead again. It was cute. *He* was cute and sexy and really smart, too. That was why she'd noticed him from the very beginning. "I don't know what to think."

He nodded and his eyes continued to draw her in, promising an answer if only she gave him a chance. "You have felt the energy. You know it is real. Come learn more tonight."

He sounded so reasonable. And the last ten minutes had shown her that her anger stemmed from another source entirely—from Joey and her uncertain future. She didn't know what to do.

"Your chi has cluttered up again," he said quietly. "Doesn't that bother you?"

She bit her lip. She did feel unsettled and…and exactly what he'd said: cluttered.

"Seven o'clock," he repeated. "Please come."

# 3

NATHAN BARELY MADE IT upstairs before he collapsed on his bed with the shakes. Sweet heaven, he hadn't realized! He hadn't known, and who could have guessed? No wonder Tracy protected herself so fiercely. No wonder she didn't date and never gave the ham-fisted American brutes the time of day. She was a tigress!

In every generation, there might be a dozen women who possessed the natural sensuality and purity to walk in the heavenly realm. These women could use their physical gifts to commune with angels and bring divine messages to Earth. It was like being a natural Buddha, only in a way most people would never accept. Buddhas used the mind to reach heaven, tigresses used their bodies as the window to the divine.

These women were a closely guarded secret in China and virtually unheard of in the United States. But he had grown up in a tigress temple, so he knew how special such women were. His great-grandmother, by all accounts, had been one of them. But the temple had floundered in recent years, in part because it lacked the guidance of a true divine tigress.

He couldn't be sure that Miss Williams was one, of course. He had only touched her chi, branded the feel of her sweet energy into his mind. But there had been such untapped power within her, that he knew... No, he corrected himself, he *guessed* at her potential.

The irony of the situation made him laugh out loud. He had just divorced himself from his homeland and left the temple never to return. He wanted nothing to do with tigresses anymore—either natural or trained. And what did he discover? Perhaps the greatest untapped spirit in his generation.

No wonder she'd seemed so innocent in their flirtations. She had to keep her natural inclinations under tight control. If a woman of such sensitivity were to accidentally awaken the tigress within her—well, that would be terrible. The sexual drives would be overwhelming. Nymphomania was the usual result. Besides, he knew she was a single parent to her brother. He doubted she had the privacy to explore her sexuality as she wanted. So she kept herself apart as a way to protect herself.

It all made sense now. But oh, how that knowledge had cost him! His organ throbbed at the memory of touching her sweet chi. What a joy it would be to slowly initiate her to the ways of the tigress, to train her to take full mastery of her sexual powers!

Except, of course, he had foresworn all that. He had left the temple and had no wish to help any tigress in any way at all. They were all selfish women focused completely on heaven at the expense of everything and everyone else. Their quest was holy, their pressures innumerable, but he was done with helping them.

He struggled with his sense of ethics. He had to explain the truth to Miss Williams. He had to tell her about the temple and her natural talents. And when she understood, she would leave for the temple in Hong Kong and he would never see her again. She wouldn't want to go, he knew, but spirits had a way of forcing a person to do things they never expected. He had seen it happen many times. An inner tigress was the most fearsome of spirits. It would want to be trained, would need to stretch for the divine. That was what tigresses did.

So whether she wished it or not, Miss Williams would end up being one of his mother's students, perhaps the brightest tigress of her generation. Nathan sighed. So much for any possibility of a relationship between himself and Tracy. Tigresses were destined for bigger things. And he...

He had to go to school, get a degree, and then earn enough money to pay for his brother's and sister's education. And, he supposed, he would do one last task for the temple. He would teach Tracy Williams about her potential. Her natural tigress spirit would do the rest. In all likelihood, she would be in China within a month.

He groaned and tried to mentally quiet his throbbing organ. How typical of his life. The moment he noticed a girl, the moment he began to pursue a fascinating and intelligent woman was also the exact moment he discovered she was beyond his reach. A tigress in Illinois! Of all the hideous, perverse luck.

Of course, he still wasn't sure, he reminded himself, but there was an easy test. She had claimed she had no interest in coming to his class tonight. If he was right, then the tigress within her would be unable to resist the call. Whether she understood it or not, she would come to him for training.

Simple. If she showed tonight, he would know she was a tigress. He would teach her the basics as quickly as possible, then send her on her way to the temple. If she didn't appear, then he would know he was wrong. He could still pursue her as a man pursued a woman. She could still be his. But only if she resisted the call...

SHE HADN'T COME. Nathan grinned as he glanced at his cell phone clock—7:10 and Tracy wasn't at class. That meant he was wrong. That meant Tracy was *not* a tigress and he could continue to pursue her. That meant at least one thing in his life was going right.

He grinned and turned to address Zoe, the only girl who had wanted to continue despite his landlord's accusations during the last class. Zoe was a sweet porcelain doll of a girl—blue eyes, blond hair, and an air of desperation about her that baffled him. Her energy was compact, tightly controlled, and a mystery that would normally intrigue him. That she was also classically Greek beautiful was an added incentive. And yet she left him cold.

But that was the best kind of student—one he could instruct without fearing any emotional connection. He smiled and turned to Zoe. "I don't think anyone else is joining us, so I guess it'll be a private lesson between us."

Zoe dimpled prettily, and Nathan began class. "As I said last time, every living thing has energy called *chi*. The male energy is called *yang*. The female is called *yin*."

A tingle sizzled down his spine, and Nathan's attention zeroed in on his apartment door. He knew without thinking that Tracy was right there, on the other side. She was hovering in indecision in the hallway, her female energy churning itself into a knot of agitation. He knew it, could sense it, and his heart sank into his toes.

He had his proof. She was a tigress. Her spirit had

forced her to come to this class, and before long, she would forget everything she was, all her earthly attachments, and pursue heaven with single-minded devotion. That was what tigresses did whether they wanted to or not, whether they willed it or not. It was their calling, and it was sacred.

A tentative knock sounded. He was already across the room, opening the door for her. She stood uncertainly in the hallway, her ball cap pulled down almost below her eyes, and his heart lurched in sympathy. He could guess how confusing this was to her. She was American and wouldn't easily believe any of it. But the spirit would not be denied.

She lifted her gaze to his, her expression equal parts nervousness and bravado. "I thought I'd watch," she said. Then she winced at the double entendre. "I mean, I need to know what's going on in my building. That's the only reason I'm here. Because I have to know what you're… what's going on here." Her voice trailed away.

He didn't respond except to step back and gesture her inside. It was all Nathan had breath to do. His eyes were devouring her. Now that he'd touched her spirit, his lust for her had grown exponentially. She'd changed from her power suit into old jeans that shaped her lovely bottom. Her top was a collared T-shirt with the symbol of the local high school embroidered just above her left breast. Her hair was tied back in a ponytail that flowed out the back of her baseball cap. All in all, she was dressed to fade into the background. Zoe in her silky stretch yoga pants and fitted crop top was the one intent on seduction. And yet everything in him yearned toward Tracy.

He bit his lip wondering at the razor-thin line he was about follow. His plan was to simply show Tracy that

Tantrism wasn't prostitution. It wasn't even necessarily erotic, depending on how one approached it. Then her calling would take over. She would demand to know more; he would provide books, guidance—and the directions to the temple in Hong Kong. Simple. Asexual.

Except he was rock hard and his every thought ran to the carnal. Why? Because she was a tigress and he was a dragon. The two powers called to one another even though she wasn't consciously aware of it. He wanted her. He would always want her. And yet she was a woman he refused to take. He was done with tigresses—Tracy included. He would simply show her the path then step aside.

He took a deep breath and gestured to the pillows on the floor. "Please," he rasped. "Please, sit down. We had just started."

She settled awkwardly, her head shrunk back into her shoulders. Her energy was skittish, tingling across his in a way that should not have been erotic. She met his gaze—only for a moment—and he wondered if she felt the same pull between them that he did. Was she already sensitive to his energy?

"Right," he said. Then he abruptly turned, taking out the elementary pictures he'd created a week ago. They were a far cry from the beautifully rendered scrolls at the tigress temple in Hong Kong. What he held up was a poster of a boy stick figure and a girl stick figure. The boy had a long dash for his dragon organ and the girl had two big circles for her lesser yin gates.

Zoe was too polite to laugh. Tracy snorted in surprise, and he smiled at her. "Artistry was never my talent."

She tightened her lips, color heating her cheeks. "I'm

sorry," she said. "It's a lovely diagram. Much better than I could do."

He nodded, momentarily entranced by the sight of her flushed expression. Her entire body seemed to lift, and her eyes sparkled. Here was the woman who'd so intrigued him over the last month: the shy flirt who seemed to shimmer with light when she smiled. But then she was gone, her face once again shielded by her baseball cap.

"All right." He tried again. "In very simplistic terms, every person has a spirit or soul. Energize that spirit enough, and one can touch the divine. There are many paths to raising the soul. Traditional Buddhists meditate themselves to the higher plane. Many live celibate, moderate lives to purify themselves. The fighting Buddhists use their physical exercises as a way to purify themselves. But the Tantrics…"

"They use sex!" chirped Zoe, obviously pleased with her burst of understanding.

"Yes," he responded automatically. "And no." His gaze inevitably slid to Tracy, but her expression was hidden, giving him no clue as to her thoughts. "Not sex. Just physical excitement."

"Orgasm." Zoe's tone was serious as she tried to sound academic.

"For the woman, yes. Her womb is like a cauldron of energy. The more it contracts in orgasm, the more it churns the energy of yin and yang combined. She can then meditate to expand that energy throughout her body and spirit and eventually…"

"Raise herself to heaven," Zoe said, her voice tightening with excitement.

"Yes."

"Yeah, right," drawled Tracy.

Nathan turned to her in silence. He wasn't stunned by her scoffing. He had heard jeering insults every day of his life. And yet, a keen sense of disappointment cut through him. Her body was here, but her mind remained resolutely closed.

The silence stretched on until she finally tilted her head back. Slowly the bill of her cap tipped enough for him to see first her light rose lips, then the tip of her nose. Eventually she straightened until he could see an apology in her eyes. "I'm sorry," she finally said. "But come on, orgasm to see God? And who does the stimulating? You?"

He settled down on his knees before her. He wore his teaching pants—loose cotton that hid the thickness of his dragon—and a light tunic on top, easily stripped away if needed. Right now it felt like the heaviest restriction across his shoulders and chest. He wanted to touch her, to show her. Instead, he kept his mind focused on his words.

"Partners are assigned later in the practice, but many have found the antechamber by their own hand."

"Alone?" squeaked Zoe from the side.

"Gives a whole new meaning to prayer vigil," Tracy quipped.

He couldn't help it. His lips quirked. "Humor is very good," he responded evenly. "Tantrism is a very human practice. And humanity requires laughter."

"And double-A batteries?"

He shrugged. "If you like." He leaned forward, allowing his own yang hunger to narrow the distance between them. "It takes practice for the male partner to sustain the female orgasm for long periods. Many of my fellow dragons resorted to mechanical means when their mouths and tongues grew tired." He let his own pride show through. "As a teen, I used to boast that I could sustain a woman for hours."

He was handling this badly. He was not a man who bragged about his accomplishments. And that was the exact worst way to speak to Tracy. He needed to be charming, to smile and ease her slowly into understanding. But he couldn't do it. His blood was running hot and hard, pushing him to show her exactly how masculine he was. He was a mature dragon, a man who would not be denied his tigress. He was worthy of her at the most primal level, and she would succumb to him.

What was wrong with him? Why was he reacting this way? Nathan took a deep breath and forced himself to think. The answer wasn't hard to come by. He had been dreaming of this woman for months. Then this morning he had touched her energy, felt her sexuality, and knew what she could be. Of course his male energy was yearning for her. Of course he wanted to stake a dragon claim on her.

But he was not a beast to be controlled by his sexual drives. He was a man who reasoned. And most of all, he was a man who knew that this woman was not for him. Unfortunately, his dragon energy didn't seem to care. Spirit went where it willed, and right now his spirit went straight for Tracy.

He leaned forward even farther, feeling his body heat with his energy. Tracy felt it, too. He could see it in the way her cheeks flushed brighter and her eyes grew wide. She started to draw away, but then froze. He waited, suspended before her, wondering what she would do next.

It came as a slow, sensuous slide of her tongue—first the pink tip, then a little more as she wet the bottom half of her full lower lip. Then she lifted her chin and smiled, baring small white teeth against her moist rosy flesh. "Bring it on, big boy," she challenged. "Prove to me this isn't some frat-boy scam."

He grinned, more than ready to accept her challenge. "Excellent." He straightened and pulled off his shirt. "It's time to learn how to purify your yin energy."

In his peripheral vision, he saw that Zoe was already stripping out of her crop top, her young pert breasts tightening in the chill air. He turned away to grab his second pathetic poster—a series of circles with stick-figure hands on them titled Purifying the Female Yin. But even as he moved, he kept his attention on Tracy, watching her blink, then gape.

Zoe had been through this once before, so she quickly shifted her legs to the proper position. She extended her left leg and pulled the heel of her right foot tight to her pleasure grotto. Then she straightened her back and set her fingertips next to the tiny buds of her nipples. She stopped there, waiting for his direction, but he was waiting for Tracy.

Would she do it? Would she take off her shirt and allow him to see what she hid under that loose T-shirt?

Not yet. She lifted her chin and smirked. "You're kidding, right?"

"Oh, get over yourself!" declared Zoe from the side. "They're just breasts. The lesser yin gates, and we massage them to open the energy flow." She turned and looked to Nathan. "We've done this before, and it feels fantastic. I could really feel my energy clear."

He nodded in approval because it was the truth. Zoe was doing well. "You don't need to do it here," he said to

Tracy. "Just memorize the pattern." He pointed at the first picture. "Circular strokes starting at the nipple then flowing outward to disperse the clogging energies."

He glanced to the side where Zoe had already closed her eyes and begun stroking herself. Her fingers weren't in the exact right position, but it seemed to be working. Her breath steadied, her shoulders straightened. And when he forced himself to attune to her surface energies, he felt that she was growing clearer as she worked.

"Very good," he said. "Now slow your strokes to time with your breath. Exhale on the downstroke, inhale on the up."

Zoe did as she was instructed while Tracy continued to stare. "Forty-nine circles," he instructed. "Use the time to calm yourself. Afterward, reverse the direction. That will stimulate your yin." Then he walked to his bookcase and pulled a primary text off the shelf. "If you need more explanation, you can borrow this book and try it in private."

He extended the heavy paperback toward Tracy, but she didn't take it. Instead, she continued to stare at him. "You really are serious," she finally whispered. "You really think this can be real."

"I have seen it. I know many who have reached the antechamber to heaven. We call it the Chamber of a Thousand Swinging Lanterns, and it is a place where orgasm becomes real, where ecstasy takes physical form." He waited a moment for her response, but she just kept staring. "Imagine a moment when orgasm suffuses not only your belly, but your heart, your soul. Every sense ripples with ecstasy, even your breath trembles with awe."

"Cool!" breathed Zoe from the side.

Tracy was shaking her head, denying everything including the book he now set in front of her. Except her left hand was trembling at the bottom of her shirt. Her body was betraying her, longing for something she couldn't allow herself to believe in.

"Miss Williams…" he began. Then he dropped on his knees in front of her. "Tracy, listen to me." If she allowed her mind to accept the possibility, then everything would go easier on her. It wouldn't change the outcome—her spirit would force her to train no matter what her mind believed—but the transition would go much smoother if she opened herself to the possibility. "You know better than anyone that this is real. You felt it this afternoon in the hallway." Her gaze snapped to his, showing fear and a trembling kind of panic.

"I—I don't know what you're talking about," she stammered.

He extended his hand, but didn't dare touch her. "I helped you clear your energy field. That is my talent. I helped you release that which confines you so you can see the truth beneath."

It was more than he had ever told anyone outside the temple, and she roundly punished him for that trust. "That's a load of crap and you know it!" she snapped.

He waited in silence, letting his field surround hers. His yang energy made his heart pound and his organ throb. How he wanted her! But he forced himself to remain still. In time, he was rewarded. Her shoulders dropped the tiniest bit.

"I'm sorry," she murmured. "That was unfair. I did feel something this morning. I just don't know what."

"I understand. Fear pushes people to do many ugly

things. Believe me, other students have said and done far worse than be rude."

She blinked. "Should I even try to understand what you're saying?"

He shook his head. "Just feel. Close your eyes." To his delight, she obeyed, her long lashes slipping down to tremble against her cheeks. "I am going to touch your face," he said. He could have taken her hands, but he wanted something more intimate. His fingers hovered just over her mouth, but then he changed his mind. She wouldn't accept a touch there. Not yet.

Extending his fingers, he brushed lifting strokes along her left cheek. She gasped as he worked, and the sound was like a hot wind blowing through his mind. It heated his yang and made his dragon surge forward. But he kept his attention on her, on the sweet feel of her chi energy as it trembled against his hand.

Another brushing stroke along her cheekbone, then he feathered his fingers against her hair. She didn't realize it, but her breath had begun to keep time with his touch: inhale with his caress, exhale as he reset. He started again, this time closer to her lips, stroking higher beside her eye and well into her hair.

His fifth stroke ended in a flick to push her ball cap off her forehead. Her eyelids fluttered so he quickly began speaking to distract her. "Do you feel the heat that builds where I touch you? That is my yang mixing with your yin. It creates heat. And passion."

She swallowed. He caught the movement at the edge of his vision, and he looked down, pleased to see that her breasts had tightened. Her body was already responding, but what about her mind? He set his fingers at the edge of her mouth, slowing his stroke even more. "Do you feel yourself becoming more centered, more calm? My strokes are pushing away that which clutters your chi."

He needed no words to strengthen his own energy. Just touching her tightened his yang to laser-point intensity. His whole body was trained on her whether he wished it so or not. Zoe slipped from his mind. The class and his plan regarding Tracy faded away, as well. All he knew was her and trying to merge his yang and her yin together. His internal fire was burning through his blood. Surely, she felt the same. It could not be this intense without both partners experiencing the flame.

"I am done throwing off your bad energies," he said in desperation, though true practice required much more time. "We will raise your good energy now, your female yin. I will make it stronger and purer." He was pushing her, moving too fast, but he couldn't stop himself. He wanted to be with her now. He wanted to feel her body and her soul quivering along with him. She had the power of a true tigress, and he was helpless against it. And he had wanted her for months now.

He lengthened his finger stroke again to finally land on her mouth. He lightly touched her bottom lip, circling his index finger there for no reason except that he wanted to. He wanted to touch the rough edges of her chapped skin, to feel the smoother—wetter—skin farther in. And then, ever so slowly, he gently inserted his finger into her mouth.

Nathan felt the wet slide of her lips followed by the rough abrasion of her teeth. And then deep inside, he touched her tongue—a push and a pull with the pad of his finger. He felt her jaw tremble beneath his knuckle and the slow curl of her tongue around him.

Without warning, his yang energy boiled over. Hot and hard, it flowed. It arrowed straight at her and plunged deep into her spirit. The energy of his mind and his body thrust into her while her lips began to move. It was not a physical merging, and yet it felt just as real, just as intense.

She narrowed her mouth and began to suck. She pulled on his finger—an instinctive move as she took his energy—but it was the most perfect feeling he had ever had. Man gave, woman received. He was pouring himself into her in a pure and smooth current.

He shuddered with the power of it. But then the experience began to change. It was still sexually enthralling, and yet it also felt like falling. He knew that his body remained exactly where it was—on the floor of his apartment, kneeling across from Tracy. But he felt as if he were plunging deep into a dark well. His skin tightened and his chest collapsed. Every inhale slowed the descent for a brief second, but then his exhale dropped him exponentially faster. Down he went into her. He knew it consciously, but the reality—the experience—was so much more terrifying. He was losing himself in her. He felt as if his body would soon collapse into a tiny dot then disappear. He would be her—completely and totally. The sexual pleasure of it was divinely intense. He was going to die, and yet a part of him didn't care.

Nathan gasped as he tried to slow the river of power— the flow of his energy from him into her. He fell backward, pulling himself away. It didn't work. His power, his male essence, continued to pour into her.

He scrambled backward, only a tiny part of his mind controlling his body's actions. The rest of him was still sinking into the divine pool that was Tracy. His hand slipped on the book he'd dropped before her and shot it across the floor. He flailed with his other hand, grabbing for an anchor—a table, a chair, a damn plastic spoon—anything to touch that wasn't her. He found it in one of his accounting textbooks. A thick hardback of cold numbers. Nothing energy-related there. And certainly nothing wet or yielding or tantalizingly female. He slammed the pages open and directed all his attention to the neat columns of figures.

And still he continued to fall. Though his eyes were trained on the figures—$12,400.00 for raw materials, $409.02 for office overhead—the better part of his mind still tumbled into her. Tracy was just now becoming aware of a change. He knew without looking that her eyes were fluttering open. She was probably dazed. Her skin would be flushed pink, her lips glossy and wet. She was so beautiful. So pure and strong…

"Wow, Nathan, you don't look so good." Zoe's words were like sandpaper across his mind. He hadn't even remembered she was there. Her words were a harsh, scraping interruption and exactly what he needed. Tossing aside his accounting text, he focused completely on Zoe. Connect to Zoe!

He couldn't do it. All he could feel was Tracy. But the act of redirecting to someone else ended the freefall. He collapsed on the carpet, but he was no longer attached energetically to Tracy. He was free, and his whole body rebelled at the thought.

"Are you all right?" Zoe asked.

Nathan nodded, though it took an effort. He coughed, using the sound to release some of the confusion inside him. He had never felt such a strong bond with anyone before. Not so that he feared he was losing himself inside her. He tried to take stock of his body. He felt weak. So weak. And his pants were wet where…

Embarrassment heated his face and he moved his arms in front of his lap. Then he steeled himself to turn back to Tracy without reestablishing the connection. As he'd expected, she was flushed pink, her mouth still slightly ajar, but her eyes were crystal clear. The dark black of her pupils had expanded, nearly drowning out the liquid brown of her irises. And in her expression he saw a raw black terror.

He knew its source even if she didn't. Her mind wasn't ready to understand what had just happened. Her body had taken his energy. The tigress inside her had eaten his strength to fuel her own growth. Her spirit had needed power and so it had taken it from him.

"T-Tracy. Miss Williams," he stammered. "I know that was confusing but—"

"Stop it!" She was on her feet, her legs obviously unsteady, but stronger than his at the moment. "Just stop it!" And with a final frightened glare at both him and Zoe, she spun on her heel and fled. He felt her every step as she pounded down the stairs. He had the strongest urge to run after her, but his legs were too weak, his mind too dazed. She had taken too much of his power. All he could do was stare at the closed door and breathe.

"What was that all about?" Zoe asked, her tone grating against his nerves.

His fingers dug into the carpet as the reality of his situation hit him hard. There was only one reason for that much power to pour suddenly and abruptly into someone's body. Only one result from what he'd just done.

Nathan pushed himself upright to settle unsteadily on his knees. It couldn't be possible. He wasn't that irresponsible. He wouldn't do that to anyone, much less the woman threatening to make him homeless. But it had happened. Without his intention, he had poured all of his power into her. And now… His belly clenched with horror. What had he just done?

"I woke her tigress," he whispered.

"Really? Awesome!" Zoe giggled. "Can you wake mine?"

He barely had the energy to laugh. "You don't understand. An uncontrolled—*untrained*—tigress can kill. It's her female energy. It's primal, it's vital, and it's awake."

Zoe frowned. "That's bad?"

"She hasn't the foggiest idea what to do with it. It's energy roiling around in her system, building and building until—"

"Orgasms for days on end?"

"No," he snapped. "Heart attack. Aneurism. Hell, her leg could spasm while she's driving and crash her into a tree. At the very least, she'll become a nymphomaniac."

Zoe was silent for a long moment, then she dipped her head in a sage nod. "Bummer."

# 4

TRACY'S CELL PHONE went off as she was driving. She cursed at the ring tone, swerved around a drunken student who'd decided to cross in the middle of the street, and nearly plowed her truck into a tree. "Yeah?" she snapped.

"Good evening to you, too, sis," drawled her brother's gravelly voice.

Tracy smiled for the first time that evening. "Hey, Joey! Done studying? Need me to pick you up?"

"Yes and no. Tommy's dad is finishing their basement and needs help with the shelving. His mom said I could stay the night if me and Tommy do the heavy lifting. She's even doing my laundry, so I got clothes. Copacetic?"

"Tommy and I," she corrected while disappointment weighted down her spirit. Still she kept her voice light. Joey didn't need his older sister tying him down even if she really hated how they'd left things this morning. "And yeah, copacetic. Though I'd really like to talk more about—"

"Cool. Bye!"

She sighed. So much for communicating with her brother. She shut her cell and directed her attention back to the road. The raw, unsettled feeling she'd had all day was stronger now, quivering inside her like a living thing. She tried to ascribe it to the strange happenings with

4C—she didn't even want to say his name—but she knew that she was fooling herself. Yeah, he had certainly exacerbated her problem. With his quiet intensity and silly stick-figure posters, he was… He was…

Hell, she didn't know what he was except that he bothered her. From the very beginning, he'd made her belly quiver and her breath skip. Why else would she start fantasizing about a tenant? But now it was so much worse. She couldn't even think about him without her toes curling in…lust? Frustration? She couldn't decide, and that bothered her even more. Perhaps she'd been fantasizing about him too much. She'd created a perfect man in her head and then wham, reality didn't meet fantasy and she ended up confused and angry.

Except, of course, reality was so much more interesting than fantasy. She'd lusted after a perfect man who catered to her every sexual whim. And wow, had she had sexual whims! Eight years worth! Then he'd walked into her apartment building, all exotic with rippling muscles and sleek black hair, and she'd had a living, breathing fantasy.

Tracy blinked, startled by her train of thought and the sudden liquid heat down low. She was getting much too worked up about his physical body. What did she think of him? She knew that what she had experienced with him this morning and this evening had been beyond amazing. This morning, her skin had tingled and her breath had felt free, as if she had been breathing through a straw all her life and suddenly got to take a deep breath.

But then she had gotten frightened and backed away. All that extra oxygen had gone to her head and freaked her out. Within moments, she had been back to her usual self but with one key difference: she remembered. She knew what it was like to take that full, deep breath and she wanted to do it again. She'd tried to block it from her mind, but couldn't. So she had gone to his class. She had to know if she had imagined everything.

It hadn't been her imagination. Tonight's experience had been beyond anything she thought possible. Not only had she breathed deeply again, but she had felt that air going to every part of her body. Every cell had popped awake. The tingling had been in her face, her arms, her *core*. Her womb had tingled, and if that wasn't cause for freaking out, she didn't know what was.

She'd lost all sense of time and place. All she'd known was Mr. Nathan Gao and the sweet wonder of a body electrified inside and out. She might have orgasmed—she wasn't even sure. It had been such a tiny piece of the overwhelming pleasure that she didn't even know.

So yes, it was real. And it all had come from Mr. Nathan Gao. So what had she done? Oh, her usual cut and run. She'd been so terrified of the experience, so overwhelmed by the sexual nature of it, that she had just bolted. Everything she'd felt was so far beyond reality that she'd had to choose: run screaming into the night or change everything she'd once believed was true. Obviously, she'd chosen option one: run screaming. But option two lingered in her thoughts. It had been real, right? She could experience it again, right?

She was halfway down Michigan Street when it happened. She'd just passed the droopy maple where Joey had fallen and broken his arm when he was eleven. The normal-ness of the memory was futilely fighting with her other memory, of Mr. Gao, when both were obliterated by a bolt of lightning.

*Tszzzz!* It fried through her thoughts and her brain, making her hands spasm on the wheel. Her foot jerked, slamming on the pedal. Fortunately, she'd been slowing down, so the lightning made her jam her foot on the brake. The truck stopped with an ugly lurch, but her face didn't. She slammed forward, her arms too numb from the lightning bolt to resist. Her face and jaw hit the steering wheel with bruising impact. She gasped, blinking as her vision flowed from stark white to black to semi-normal again.

At least the air bag hadn't deployed. In truth she hadn't done anything but slam on the brakes for no reason at all, but she felt as if she'd just been in a ten-car pileup. Tracy sat there in the middle of the road, breathing deeply, feeling her jaw throb, and…

Wow. She tingled all over. Serious tingling with a side of throbbing, and not just in her face. 4C zipped into her thoughts, and just like that, her breasts tightened, her belly quivered, and lower down… Wow. She seriously needed to get a grip. A zillion fireflies were zipping through her system, firing up the most inappropriate places.

She took a deep breath, trying to settle her nerves. Unfortunately, that only rubbed her breasts against her shirt, setting off another firestorm of sensations. Jeez, what was that? It was like a lightning strike of the hornies.

Mr. Gao was still in her thoughts, only now her imagination made him naked. She could see his rippling muscles as clear as day, lean and perfectly sculpted. Then the two of them were in his bedroom, and he was promising to do amazing, erotic things to her. It was just how she'd fantasized a zillion times. Except this time, she wasn't in the privacy of her bedroom, she was in her truck in the middle of the street! Without her wanting it, her breath shortened, her pelvis shifted on the seat, and the throbbing lower down deepened into a bass drum.

No, no, no! Not here! Clenching her jaw, she mentally obliterated all thoughts of Mr. 4C. Whatever weird energy thing he'd done to her, she was in control of her body. She would not succumb to this…this echo of whatever. It was not real. And even if it felt real, it was just temporary. Lightning-bolt intense, but very, very temporary.

Gripping the steering wheel, Tracy pressed down on the accelerator. Her truck leaped forward with an ominous grind. Fortunately, she wasn't far from home. Minutes later, she pulled into her garage without any more throbbing. No less throbbing, but no new lightning strike of the hornies. She counted that as a win.

Her legs were weirdly steady—energized even—as she bounded out of the truck and into the house. She reached to flip on the lights, but then remembered that Joey wasn't sleeping here tonight. No need to give the place that welcome feel.

She made it up the stairs quickly, slipped past her brother's room, ignored as always the shut door of her parents' old room, and careened into her own. Her nerves were zinging so much her hair felt as if it was standing on end. She banged on the overhead light only to curse and cut it off again.

She didn't want the harsh glare. She wanted muted half light and sexy saxophone music as she slid her clothing off. She bounced across the room and flipped on her bedside lamp. It was a silly pink thing surrounded by clowns. She'd had it from when she was a baby and rarely looked at it. But right then it gave her room the perfect soft glow.

Then she focused on her pink eyelet curtains—another childhood leftover—and imagined herself in a lush boudoir stripping for a lover. 4C was just behind her, watching from her bed, his dark Chinese eyes drinking in her every move. He was naked except for those black cotton pants that rested ever so tantalizingly low over his hips, and he was waiting for her.

The first thing she did was strip off her ball cap and shake out her ponytail. Whatever possessed her to wear that stupid thing anyway? It was too restrictive and held everything too tight. How luxurious it felt to dig her fingers deep into her scalp and then shake out her hair.

The brown waves would have felt good on her back, but the tight band of sports bra beneath her T-shirt prevented any sensation. Normally she would have ripped the shirt right off, tossing it into the laundry bin with a perfect two-point shot. Not tonight. Not with her fantasy lover watching from the bed and her hips gyrating from some music she felt but couldn't hear.

She wrapped her arms around her stomach and slowly lifted her shirt. It wasn't the smoothest motion in the world, but she didn't care as the fabric tugged against her back. Yup. Tingles. Still there. Still waiting to be awakened by a brush of fingertips, a stroke of lips, or the much less glorious pull of cotton.

It didn't matter. Tracy tugged it off, already impatient to be free. The sports bra was harder. It clung so stubbornly to her body that she had to peel it away. The feel on her breasts was like thick plastic being lifted off to reveal a younger, perkier her. But that was nothing compared to the sensation of her nipples pebbling in the cool night air. When they tightened, her belly did, too, which set off those tingles, which swirled though her entire system enough to make her brain sweat.

Oh, my! She fell forward, landing hard on the mattress. She had to get naked now! Flopping over, she yanked off her jeans while those tingles began zipping everywhere at random. Her toes curled; her thigh spasmed; and her nose itched.

"9-1-1," she gasped to no one at all. "I've been struck by horny lightning and I can't get off!" She started to giggle but that only created more explosions of hunger. It wasn't just her skin firing random patches of heat, but inside, as well. She swore even her spleen was quivering with desire.

The ring of her cell phone rumbled through the room. It would have been jarring if the deep notes didn't resonate with her on a very intimate level. But the rhythm was too fast or not fast enough, so she scrambled—gasping—across her bed to her discarded jeans and the cell phone inside. It was thick and hard in her fingers as she gripped it, but way too narrow. She cursed as she flipped it open, wanting something very different in her hands.

"What?" she gasped, startled to realize that the word had come out breathy and seductive. What if it was her brother calling?

"Miss Williams? Is that you?"

Not Joey. Sexy Mr. Gao. Didn't his name just roll through her system in absolute perfection? "Gaaaaooow," she purred. "Mr. Gaaaaooooww, did you need something?"

He said a word in Chinese. It was low, guttural and completely at odds with her mood.

"What?" she said as she flipped onto her back and

lifted her breasts to the ceiling. She had no understanding of why she did that. It just felt right.

"I'm so sorry, Miss Williams."

"Tracy," she whispered. "Call me Tracy." She closed her eyes, lifting her hand to trail the very edges of her nails across her collarbone, curving across her left breast, to flick—ah!—hard against her nipple. "Hmmmm."

"How are you feeling, Tracy? How does your body feel, right now?"

*Naked. I feel naked.* "I'm fine, Mr. Gaaaaooooow." She flicked her nipple again, enjoying the spark of tingles that burst across her flesh.

"Listen to me, Tracy, I think I woke your tigress. Your inner tigress—it's awake."

"Me-yowrrrr, Mr. Gaaaooowww." Had she just said that aloud?

Dead silence. It lasted long enough for her to lift the phone away to see if she'd lost the connection. She hadn't, so she brought the receiver back to her ear.

"Hellooooooo?" she cooed.

"Listen very closely, Tracy. You need to… You've got energy firing all through your body."

*Too right,* she purred silently to herself.

"You're going to have to learn how to control it, to dampen it until you can get some training. I'm serious Tracy. You're risking your life."

She frowned. Her thoughts had finally filtered past his sexy voice to actually hear his words. What he said wasn't pleasant at all. She pulled her hand away from fondling her nipple and made a valiant effort to focus. "What?"

"You need training, Tracy. Or you're not going to be able to control your actions." He sighed, the low rumble

of air somehow making her toes curl in delight. "Nymphomania is the usual result. You don't want to become
a nymphomaniac, do you?"

Tracy rolled over onto her stomach in an attempt to
focus, but automatically extended the motion, lifting her
tush high in the air, feeling the cool air hit her wet thighs.
Oh, to have him behind her right now.

"I am not a nymphomaniac," she said, irritated not by
the suggestion but because he wasn't behind her, thrusting hot and hard inside her. She'd dreamed of such a
thing for so long.

"Think, Tracy. Is this your usual behavior? Is this how
you usually feel?"

Her mind reeled a moment. What was she doing? She
plopped down flat on the cover and glared at her bedside
table. "No," she said slowly. "Not really." But it wasn't
completely unusual, either. After all, she had been doing
this with him in her dreams for weeks now.

The war between logic and lust collided in her brain,
short-circuiting any rational thought. She understood
nothing of what was going on, couldn't focus to save her
life, and was talking to a studly man who was not, not,
not seducing her!

"You listen here," she said, her tone sharpening. "I'm
alone in my own home, and I can do whatever I want!"
She sat up and glared at her tousled, flushed face in the
mirror. She knew she had completely lost it here, and yet
she couldn't stop herself. With a grunt of frustration, she
slammed the phone shut and threw it across the room.

Almost before it landed, the ring tone rumbled through
the room. Mr. Gaaaooow, again, she was sure. The low
notes strummed her insides. She tried to ignore it, but she

couldn't. With another curse, she flounced across the room and flipped it open.

"—Tracy!"

"What?" She'd dropped to all fours on the floor to grab the phone, and her breasts swung with abandon. If she crouched a bit more, she could rub her nipples across the carpet. It was rough, not even remotely what she wanted, but it still felt good. Not great, but good.

"Tracy! You need to release some of your energy."

She'd dreamed of his hands on her breasts. Big hands, hard hands. Pulling. Sucking. Twisting her nipples. Her fantasy took on a life of its own and she forgot that she was still holding the phone. She didn't remember until one of her moans sparked a response from him.

"That's good, Tracy. You need to fantasize something. Pretend I'm there. Pretend I'm biting you. Little nibbles along your neck and down to your breasts. I'm biting your nipples, Tracy. And I'm sucking them into my mouth. They're stretching, Tracy. Pull on your nipples, feel the stretch, and then pinch. That's my teeth biting you."

For all that his words were just what she wanted to hear, his tone was more like a radio announcer giving the weather. She pulled the phone away from her ear intending to toss it aside, but she couldn't quite make herself do it. She wanted to hear more. She wasn't going to do what he said, but she wanted to hear.

She groaned, low and in the back of her throat. Then she looked down at herself and was startled to realize she was doing exactly what he said. She was fondling herself. Whenever she'd done this before it had been a sneaky movement, under her covers and with a great deal of guilt. But not this time. This time she felt free to touch herself openly.

She took a deep breath and widened her legs. Wow, did this feel good.

"Are you there, Tracy? Tracy?"

"It's never felt right before," she gasped as she touched her breast again. "It's felt embarrassing. But now I've got this tingling and I can breathe and it feels great!"

"That's your tigress. She's awake now." Then his voice dropped to a lower register. Not quite the sexy murmur she'd dreamed of, but very nice. Verrrrrrrrry nice indeed. "Touch yourself lower, Tracy."

Her hand was already there, pushing into herself. Her legs were trembling, her hand was pinching and pushing, but it wasn't what she wanted. "It feels so empty," she gasped. Then her body started convulsing. Orgasmic contractions rippled through her. They went on and on, and it felt good—but also blank. She had no other word for it. Blank contractions like a muscle spasm or a repetitive sneeze. A release but unsatisfying at the same time.

Without understanding why, she curled on her side and began to cry. Tiny sobs intertwined with orgasmic gasps. "I've gone insane," she whimpered. "I'm completely insane."

"No, you're not," Mr. Gao said through the phone. His voice was soothing, stroking a part of her deep inside. "You're not insane. That's what I've been trying to tell you. You've just been awakened and that's a scary, confusing thing."

"It's wonderful," she sobbed, not even knowing why she cried. "I can breathe."

"I'm almost there, Tracy. Open the door for me, okay?

I'm almost to your house. I got your address from Mrs. Ludlow in 1B. We'll talk. I'll explain."

The lust was cooling, allowing room for rational thought. She was curled naked on the floor after having brought herself to orgasm while on the phone. On the phone! What had she done?

"Tracy? Can you unlock the door for me?"

She closed her eyes, humiliation washing through her. "No," she whispered. "No, I can't." Then she turned off her cell.

# 5

"Tracy? It's Nathan Gao. Don't be afraid."

Her favorite fleece blanket settled across her body. She was still curled on her floor, her mind resolutely blanked to everything that was happening. Except the blanket did feel very nice. She had been a little cold.

"I'm going to pick you up now. You'll be more comfortable on the bed."

She frowned into the crook of her elbow. She was an independent woman. She could get up all by herself. Except his hands felt wonderful as they gently worked themselves under her thighs and shoulders, then lifted her off the floor. Without intending to, she snuggled against his shoulder, hiding her face as she smelled his wonderful scent. Spice, ginger and something else bypassed her brain and settled deep into her womb. What was it? A musk that was all male and made the back of her throat purr. She burrowed deeper against him, appreciating the hard ridges of his pectorals at her face and the full bulge of his biceps beneath her thighs.

But then he set her down. He was excruciatingly gentle as he lay her head on her pillow. She didn't want to let him go, but her hands were tangled in her blanket and she couldn't reach him fast enough.

"I'm going downstairs," he said. "I've brought some tea that will help cool your yin. Then we can talk."

"How did you get in the house?" That wasn't at all what she wanted to ask. She was thinking other things entirely—like how could she possibly be embarrassed about the situation while simultaneously wanting to throw off the blanket and jump him? It was a simmering-in-the-background kind of urge, but she felt it nonetheless.

"I ran here," he answered. "And then I…uh…I picked the lock." His skin darkened to a dusky red, but his eyes were unapologetic. "I was afraid for you."

"What's happening to me?" Her voice came out surprisingly steady given that she really wasn't sure she wanted to know the answer.

He ran a distracted hand through his hair, standing it up in spiky points. "I woke your inner tigress. Some people call it your kundalini."

She blinked, forcing her mind to focus on his words, not just the movement of his lips and how they would feel against her skin. "I, uh…I think you better go make that tea. I'll get dressed and meet you downstairs."

He nodded, his shoulders dropping an inch with the movement. "Good. That's good. We'll—"

"Talk. Yes, I think that would be very good. Talk." Away from her bed. With clothing on. "Coffee. Strong, hot coffee."

"You will like my tea better," he said, and then he was gone. But not before she saw that he wore a different pair of teaching pants, these made of faded black cotton that outlined his muscular bottom and could be undone with a single yank on the tie. Yup, the horny fireflies were still zipping around her system, giving her thoughts that made her blush.

She frowned as she watched him leave. She'd never had thoughts like this before. Fantasies—yes. Vivid pretense—yes. But a powerful urge to have a man—this particular man—thick and hard inside her? Never. A wetness inside and out that made her so needy she wanted to jump out of her skin? Not once.

Tracy made a concerted effort to tamp down these bizarre urges as she extricated herself from bed. Then she grabbed her most asexual clothing—loose sweatpants and an even looser T-shirt—and headed downstairs. She made it into her kitchen just as the whistle began to blow on the teakettle. She watched him from the doorway, seeing his hand—large, long fingers wrapping firmly about the dark handle—lift the kettle and pour steaming water into two mugs. The steam rose, wrapping about his face just as he looked up.

Dark eyes pierced her straight through. It was a physical connection that pulled her straight into the kitchen, to his side and then into his arms. She was raising her lips to his mouth long before her mind thought to object.

She felt his hand wrap around her back, and those long fingers slipped underneath her T-shirt to fire across her back. She shivered in delight and lifted up on her toes. Her lips tingled; her belly tightened. He was so close, she could see the way his eyes darkened with hunger. He wanted her; she knew it. And yet just before their lips touched, he drew away and pressed a steaming mug of tea to her mouth.

"Drink," he ordered.

"No—" He tilted the mug and she had to sip or let it spill down her front. She pulled away as soon as she could. "I don't want tea." She wanted him. But he was holding her firmly away.

"Drink," he ordered again.

She did, not because she wanted to but because there was such strength in his tone. He had the most manly voice she'd ever heard. So she wrapped her hands around his on the mug and sipped. She kept her touch seductive—a caress that slowly enveloped. She savored the hard bones of his hand and the smooth expanse of skin over long tendons. His every knuckle pressed into her palm while she held his gaze, seeing the dark pupils of his eyes expand. She pursed her lips again, this time making every sip a seduction.

Beneath her fingers, his hand trembled. She felt more than heard the groan that rumbled through his body. "You must try to control yourself. Your tigress is very strong, but your mind is stronger."

She didn't want to hear him. She was close enough to smell his scent. He had run over here, but his sweat wasn't rank. It was a clean kind of smell. Exotic. Like spiced cucumber. She closed her eyes to better appreciate it. Instead, she heard his ragged inhale as he stepped backward, gently withdrawing his touch from her.

Tracy shifted, releasing him while keeping hold of the mug. She sipped again, noticing for the first time that the brew was spicy. Not sweet. She liked sweet. "This tastes like…" She abruptly sneezed. "Peppered, dirty water." She took another sip, then another, beginning to like the bite against the back of her throat. She tasted ginseng and… "Is there pepper in this?"

"Cayenne."

She took another deep drink as she shifted to sit at the kitchen table. "It's good in a weird kind of way. What exactly is it?"

He joined her at the table, folding himself precisely into the chair. She met his eyes across the rim of her mug, seeing both apology and fear in his expression. Anxiety trembled across her spine, and she slowly set down her empty mug.

"What?"

"Your female energy has been awakened," he said clearly. "It is flooding your body, giving you thoughts and feelings you—"

"Horny lightning," she said, speaking more to herself than to him. "The tingles. The thoughts. That's my female energy?" She didn't want to believe him, but what he said explained the events of the last hour. Had she been on the floor? "Is there more tea?"

He nodded, crossing efficiently to his worn attaché case that she now noticed leaning against her cabinets. He drew out a metal cylinder with one hand while grabbing the kettle with the other. Within moments, he was dropping a fine powder mixed with thin dried leaves into her mug. The steam from the kettle curled about the hard angles of his face while he poured, and she felt her belly quiver at the sight.

This wasn't good. She shouldn't be thinking of steam baths, hot sprays, naked pulsating flesh. "I've never been like this." To distract herself, she grabbed the tea container, reading the label with all the focus she could muster. "Advanced Men's Virility Formula? You're giving me Chinese Viagra?"

"You have too much yin," he answered calmly as he tried to pull the tin out of her hand.

She shifted it out of his reach, turning to read the list of ingredients. "Oh, my—" She choked off her next word. "Do you know what the primary ingredient is?"

"You need more yang to balance out your yin—"

"Horny goat weed."

"Yang is male energy. It will balance your energies. Too much yin requires more yang to stabilize—"

"Look right here." She pointed to the list. "Horny goat weed!"

He lifted it out of her hand. "And it is making you feel better." He pushed her full mug at her. "So drink."

She stared at him, trying to hold on to her righteous indignation. She couldn't. She did feel thirsty. She lifted the mug and inhaled the steam. "I can't believe I'm drinking this stuff."

He set the tin back on the table. "Keep it. Drink as much of it as you want."

"I can't keep that stuff here! What if my brother sees it?"

He held her gaze. "What if your brother sees you as you were an hour ago?"

Her face heated. Had she really purred his name?

His hand circled hers on the table—large, enveloping and so strong. "Don't be embarrassed. Understand what is happening."

"This will wear off, right? I mean, it'll go away."

"Do you really want it to?"

"Yes!" Panic was making her chest tighten. She looked down and noticed that she'd flipped her hand over and was now gripping his. There was a tingle where their palms met, a flow of heat and serenity that whispered up her wrist into her arm. "What are you doing?" she cried. She wanted to leap away, but it felt too good.

"You need more yang to balance the yin," he answered. "I am giving you mine. Or what little is left of it."

"Your what?"

"My male power. I am giving you mine. Don't you feel how it makes you more balanced?"

She quieted a moment, trying to feel. It was hard. Her heart was beating triple time and her breath stuttered in and out in rapid puffs.

"Quiet your mind. Your body will follow," he instructed.

She swallowed, trying to do what he wanted. But her mind was racing. This couldn't be happening to her. It was a scam. She'd been drugged. She'd drunk his tea. What was going on?

She heard him huff in frustration, then a movement. Her eyes shot open a split second before it happened. She saw his face so close, and then he was kissing her. The motion was so sudden, the action so unexpected that at first all Tracy could do was gasp in surprise. But then she felt a surge of heat against her lips and the stroke of his tongue as he penetrated her mouth. She opened herself to him—to his power as he filled her, to his thrust even as she began to meet him, to toy with him. Her belly tightened, her blood surged, and between one heartbeat and the next, she had absolute clarity of thought. She wanted him. *Now.*

Then he pulled away. "Listen carefully and quickly," he said, his voice thick and raw. "This passion is yours. It is clear and powerful, and it can consume you. But your sexuality is your right. Do you really want to throw it away?"

"No. God, no!" She had never felt so alive. She was aware of everything. Her breath as it filled her lungs, the heat in her face, the position of her thighs. Other details appeared with stark clarity, as well: the angular cut of his jaw, the way his button-down shirt was undone at the collar revealing smooth skin, the jut of his Adam's apple.

"I stopped thinking of boys—of men—when my parents died. There wasn't time for that. But lately…" From the moment she'd met him, she'd started fantasizing again. She'd started thinking of being a woman again. It was time. She'd lost so much when her parents had died.

"Good," he answered softly. "It is good to be a whole woman, isn't it?" Then he leaned forward. "Let me teach you how to control this power."

"Yes." She abruptly grabbed his arms to pull him even closer. "Yes, I want to learn everything. Right now, Nathan. I want to do it all!"

## 6

"TAKE OFF YOUR TOP," he said. "You must do the breast circles. That will help clarify and calm your yin energy."

Tracy didn't want to hesitate—she'd made her decision—but doubt still made her hands tremble. She looked into Mr. Gao's eyes—a virtual stranger—and saw no softening in his expression. He merely challenged her to carry through.

She did. She stripped off her T-shirt. She hadn't even put on a bra since the very idea had felt too confining. And now she breathed deeply. She let her lungs expand, lifted her breasts, and tried to be completely at ease with being half-naked in her kitchen across from an enigmatic stranger.

"We will begin with your breath."

When he spoke, his voice sounded absolutely calm, even a little bored. But when she looked into his eyes, she knew he was far from serene. His gaze held hers with laser-point intensity, and she shuddered in reaction.

"Place your fingers near your nipples. Use three fingers and spiral them outward."

An image of Zoe and her young, perky breasts flashed through her mind. Tracy straightened her back and felt her bulbous size Cs jiggle. She had always thought she had good-looking breasts—assuming they were appropriately lifted and shaped in a fifty-dollar Victoria's Secret bra. But hanging free, they tended to…well, hang.

She sneaked a glance at Mr. Gao and wondered what he thought of her most feminine attribute. She was a lot larger than most Chinese girls. Was that a good thing? His expression gave no clue to his thoughts, but his gaze was trained on her chest.

"Size and shape are unimportant," he said as if reading her thoughts. "I have seen old breasts and young ones, large and small, wrinkled and removed, even ones sculpted by the most gifted plastic surgeons." He lifted his eyes to hers. "Beauty, joy, and most especially feminine power is a thing of the mind and of the energy. Do you wish to hone yours?"

"Yes," she answered immediately. Such was the power of his focused attention she would have said yes to anything.

"Then be done with this self-consciousness. It is tedious."

She blinked, startled by his cold tone. Didn't he understand how hard this was for her? How confusing? She closed her eyes and tried to focus, but her hands still trembled where she placed them on her breasts.

Then she heard him sigh—the sound filled with very male frustration. "Give me your hand," he said.

She blinked, completely confused. Then before she could react, he grabbed hold of her wrist and pulled it toward him. He was sitting across from her on an old wooden kitchen chair. His legs were braced wide apart, the soft cotton fabric of his pants stretched taut.

"You are beautiful, Tracy. But you hide yourself under ugly clothing and an angry exterior."

"I'm not angry!"

He kept talking as if she hadn't spoken. "But I see you

clearly, Tracy. I see your beauty and your sexuality." He leaned forward, his grip on her wrist too strong for her to pull away. "I see you, Tracy."

He pushed her hand against his groin. His knees had narrowed enough for his pants to grow slack, but what she touched was anything but soft. He was hard. Iron-rod hard. Nothing so sleek or cool as steel. He was rough, powerful and thick against her palm, radiating a heat that drew her ever closer.

She had never touched a man like this before. The closest she'd gotten was the dildo her friend had given her on her twenty-first birthday. This felt so solid, so alive. She wanted to grip him, to take that life into herself, to do all those things she'd heard about but never done.

Then Nathan pulled her hand away. "That is the last time you will touch me, Tracy."

Her gaze leaped to his face. "What?"

"Now you know I desire you. Your tigress energy calls to my dragon power. But you are not strong enough to meet me on an equal plane." His voice dropped to a softer tone. "You are not ready, Tracy, and you never will be if you continue to doubt yourself and me."

Unexpected tears welled up in her eyes. "I don't understand any of this."

"There is no need to try," he answered. "For the moment, simply breathe." He returned her hand to her breast, adjusting her fingers to press the inside edge of each nipple. "Now begin to spiral. Inhale on the upstroke, exhale on the down."

He guided her hands, drawing them up and around her breasts. Each circle expanded, moving ever wider until she ended all the way underneath, stroking ribs as much as breast. Then he took her hands back to the beginning.

"Start again. Feel your breath flow in and out. Let it follow the stroke of your hands."

"What does this do?" she whispered.

"It disperses your clogging energies. You are circulating your chi, throwing off negative energy. With every exhale, it leaves. With every inhale you draw in pure, sweet truth."

She cracked her eyes, part of her wondering if he had actually said that with a straight face. He caught her glance, of course, and arched his eyebrow at her. It was a challenge—clear as day—and yet all she could think was that he was a beautiful, beautiful man.

"This will make me ready for you? For us to meet on an equal plane?" She didn't have to elaborate as to what plane she referred to. She meant the horizontal, in bed, having fabulous sex plane, and he knew it. God, when did she start having thoughts like that?

His expression sobered. "It is one step on the path. Tracy, you and I will never be together. I am your teacher. We will never partner. That will be for another dragon, selected by you and the temple from an eligible pool of candidates."

She frowned. "A temple? There's a temple that studies sex?"

"Yes, in Hong Kong. I grew up there."

She wasn't sure if he meant that he grew up in Hong Kong or in a temple that studied sex. But there wasn't time to ask as he leaned forward onto his knees, pressing his words into her as firmly as she pressed her fingers against her skin.

"And this is not about having sex. This is about maximizing your possibilities. You have taken a huge step—your tigress is awake. Your possibilities are endless."

"Except you're not one of those possibilities," she said, her heart sinking to her toes.

"No, I'm not." Was there regret in his gaze? She couldn't tell. And before she could ask, he touched the back of her wrist. "Think only of now. Breathe."

She obeyed because she always did when he spoke in that tone. It was his dragon power, she supposed, and she couldn't fight it. So she closed her eyes and tried to concentrate as she moved her hands in a rough spiral. Inhale. Exhale. The refrigerator kicked on with an audible hum. It didn't sound right. Just how old was that thing anyway? Would she have to replace it soon? How was she going to afford that?

She was supposed to be thinking about her breasts. They were just breasts. She moved her hands again. Kinda felt like a nice breast exam. Her friend Mary had recently had a mammogram. Her experience had been awful.

She heard another sound. Or was that a puff of air across her face? She was surprised that she didn't feel cold—

"Bring your thoughts back to here."

Tracy jumped and spun around. He'd spoken right behind her ear. How had she not heard him move? He knelt behind her, his arms wrapped around the chair back and her body, all without touching her.

"How do you move so quietly?" she demanded.

"I walk with my chi."

"Of course, Grasshopper," she drawled, completely unnerved by his presence. Now that she knew he was there, she felt his heat enveloping her, his breath as it whispered through her hair and tickled her cheek. "Can you—"

"Shh. Close your eyes and begin again." He placed his hands over hers.

"I thought we weren't ever going to touch." Her voice trembled. And those fireflies were buzzing back to life.

"*You* aren't going to touch me again. I will have to touch you. Especially since you have no experience in quieting your thoughts. Be here. Completely. Now."

No choice, given how he had wrapped himself around her. His breath tickled, but it was his hands that held her attention. They were so large compared to hers, cupping around hers to join her fingertips at her breasts.

"Inhale," he whispered.

She did. Her chest lifted into where he held her fingers. She touched—they touched—the skin right beside her nipples. Then he began to move her hands, spiraling them up and around. It felt so different from when she did it herself. His fingers seemed to extend not only around hers, but deep into her skin, as well. It was his heat, but it felt like so much more. Strength. Flow. Chi. Names filtered through her consciousness only to be scattered as they began the downstroke along the sides of her breasts.

His power preceded where their fingers moved. It slipped into her skin, lifting her breasts and opening them in ways she couldn't imagine. She had expected the trailing fire of pressure behind their hands, but his strength pushed ahead and penetrated deep.

They circled again under her breasts, lifting so that his wrist accidentally flowed across her left nipple. Lightning shot through her chest straight to her womb, and her entire body shuddered. Beside her, she felt him gasp, as well, his arms jolting where they rested across her upper arms.

Then she heard him swallow. "Your tigress nips at me with her claws," he whispered.

"I want to jump the nearest ready cock," she murmured

back, stunned that she wasn't joking. Of course, the nearest cock was his.

He smiled. She felt his cheek lift against the edge of her ear and she heard laughter in his tone. "Many are ready, all will be willing," he said, "but they will not satisfy you."

"Why not?"

"Because the answer is here." He pushed her hands into movement again. "In your own hands."

"And in my bedside table." An obvious joke, but she couldn't resist. He made her nervous.

"In clarity," he corrected. "Focus on what we are doing."

As if she could do anything but feel him surround her, know that it was his hands guiding hers, and live each breath wishing they could continue what they were doing forever.

"Breathe," he murmured, the low vibration of his word penetrating almost as deeply as his heat.

She inhaled with his upstroke. Exhaled with his down. Then another circle and her breasts felt like changed things. They were still breasts, but they were also energy—calm, quiet and very, very there. Like bright, golden little mounds on her chest, alive and new. She wanted to speak, she wanted to express how wonderful this was, but she feared breaking the spell. Each stroke made her chest—no, her whole body—a little brighter.

He lightened, as well. The weight of his arms on hers disappeared. Instead, he became part of her, an extension of her body. She knew his temple pressed against hers, and his chest brushed up tight to her back, but there was no added weight. There wasn't even the fire that she had expected. He was simply part of her, and together they breathed as one, moved as one.

"Forty-nine," he said. The sound blended into the air, folding around her without surprise or disharmony. "Those strokes dispersed the negative. Now we will awake the positive."

"I thought my tigress was already awake."

"Wait and feel."

He held her hands by her sides. But this time, instead of curving under her breasts, he stroked over the top. She still inhaled as he moved, lifting her breasts into their joined hands. And as they spiraled in toward her nipples, she felt herself relax into total trust.

She would wait and see. And in waiting, she felt life pouring into her body and her breasts. She had no other word for it. She was alive before, but now she was *alive!* Or at least her breasts were. Before, her body had been a beautiful glowing landscape of serenity. Now that landscape was being stroked into Technicolor brilliance. She no longer felt hot. Though there was a blaze of hunger under her flesh, she expanded past her skin. She was wondrously, gloriously more. More awake, more alive, more *here* than ever before. And it was all from his touch. The circles continued, but her hands slipped away. She wanted him to touch her; she wanted his hands on her body.

His fingertips were larger than her own; they widened the gentle pressure on her skin and deepened the stroke of his energy. She felt him all the way to her spine. He was heat that had little to do with temperature—caressing her, stroking her.

"Yes," she whispered. "Oh, yes."

But after a few more spirals, she felt a growing discontentment. His spirals always ended near her nipples without touching them. He stroked her higher and hotter with each spiral, but would not quite reach the peak.

"More," she whispered.

"Isn't this enough?" he countered, humor lacing his voice. "Do you feel how your breath boils with fire?"

It did. She did. Every exhale released steam. Every inhale brought more oxygen to the blaze, but it wasn't enough. Her hands had fallen away, down by her sides. With only the tiniest movement, she extended them backward so that she gripped his thighs.

He was crouched behind her, his legs braced on either side of her chair. She could reach—and massage—the corded muscles behind her, tightening her hands with his every stroke.

"You are not supposed to touch your teacher," he said.

"Then stop me."

He didn't, though she felt the conflict within him. Then she began to move with his strokes. As he circled her breasts, she drew her hands higher on his thighs. At first it was a small movement, a simple shift of her wrists. But as he continued to flow around and around her breasts, she began to lengthen her movements. She extended her arms and grabbed him just above his knees.

His muscles were clearly defined there. The thin cotton fabric did nothing to disguise the lean strength of him. She knew she could grip her hands as tightly as possible and he would barely notice. She began with a grip, but as his thighs widened, her hands opened, making her touch more of a caress.

His arms tightened. The chair back creaked as he leaned harder against it, more fully into her. He no longer touched her with just the pads of his fingertips, but the full lengths of his fingers. And though he was careful not to touch her nipples, more and more of her breasts hummed beneath his stroke.

"Focus on the energy," he whispered. "This is not sexual—"

"Shh," she interrupted. His words were disruptive. Yes, she felt the energy expanding all around them. She was her body, but also so much more. And together, they were like a bright flame of light.

And contrary to what he claimed, it was also very sexual. Her breasts were pulsing with power that throbbed on a direct line to her womb. Even better, that beat seemed to echo through their joined energy, reverberating in her mind and through her hands where she stroked his thighs.

"Touch me," she whispered.

"This is not sexual," he began.

"Touch me!" she ordered, and she felt power echo through the words. Then at the peak of her stroke, she stretched one hand farther up so that she had his cock in her grasp.

She heard him gasp in alarm, and his hips jerked in reaction, but he didn't move away. His body thrust forward into her palm and in that moment, she knew she had won. He had his dragon power, a force she didn't even begin to understand, but apparently, she had her own strength. She could touch him, she could hold him and feel the heat of him like a sun. It arrowed through her hand all the way up her arm. It stroked across her palm, allowing her to measure the length and girth of him. And most of all, it allowed her to wrap her fingers around him and keep him right there, hard and hot.

She let her head fall back against his shoulder and wished that they didn't have a hard wooden chair between them. Then she simply breathed, letting her lungs expand into his hands as they now spread around her full breasts, cupping them as a man would. He held her now, without circles, without intention, he simply held her as she held him.

"What now, Grasshopper?" she asked.

"The tigress wants to play, does she?" he answered, his voice a seductive caress.

"She does." She pulled her hand upward a bit so that she could roll her forefinger across his tip. She felt the wetness in his pants and knew he trembled behind her.

"Then lean forward into my touch and spread your legs."

She did, but she was still wearing her sweatpants. They felt hot and confining, but when Tracy shifted her free hand to release them, he tightened his arm, holding her still.

"But my pants—"

"I am going to penetrate you with my energy, Tracy. I will not touch you more than I am now, but my chi will. My masculine dragon power will dance in your cave until you quiver your delight. In this way, you will know it is real."

"Really?" she asked, fear and excitement building inside her. "Is that really possible?"

She felt his face turn toward her neck, and then his lips pressed against her, right at the pulse point beneath her jaw. "Not only is it possible, Tigress Tracy, but it is only the beginning."

She thought about telling him then. She thought about confessing how new all of this was. Sure the energy stuff was very unique, but did she tell him that no man had ever… That she had never…

His hands began to move again, and her thoughts scattered. Whatever she had done—or not done—in the past didn't make a difference. This was about now, and she didn't want it to stop. She wanted to learn what she had been missing all those years. And so she closed her mind to her other thoughts and let herself experience this.

His hands circled around her breasts, spiraling around until they nearly reached her nipples, but this time it felt different. This time, there was a dangerous tension in his movements. As if he really was a dragon wrapping around her body.

His hands tightened—not painfully but deeply. She was sure he could feel her ribs beneath her breasts, but his energy went further. It slipped around her nipples to coil inside her chest. With every pulsing compression from his hands, his power pushed deeper, like a living flame tunneling straight through her.

Beneath her hand, she felt his penis come alive, as well. It seemed to move, twisting and shifting in an echo of what she felt inside her. She heard his breath, deep and long, heating the skin at her neck, over her collarbone and down around her breasts. All was movement and flame—in her hand, deep in her chest, and rolling over her skin.

"What is that?" she whispered.

"Yang power. Refined, purified, and aimed like an arrow shot from a bow."

"Aimed where?" she whispered, though she knew the answer.

"To you. To your core, Tigress."

"I've never…" The words slipped out, but then were cut off in a gasp of surprise. He nipped the back of her neck. A shiver expanded from the sharp bite of sensation, only to be followed by waves of desire as his wet tongue stroked her skin. "Wow. Do that again."

His lips curved into a smile. "Do not seek to instruct the dragon on how to stalk his prey."

He squeezed her nipples—finally!—a single sharp twinge of sensation. Her thoughts had been on her neck, so the bolt of lightning caught her unawares, sizzling down that invisible cord to her womb and up another line straight into her brain. She couldn't seem to catch her breath. She was leaning forward as he had instructed, but now she arched her back, curving her pelvis such that her inner core pressed down against the seat.

"Lean your head forward," he whispered, this time from farther behind her ear.

She did, and her hair slipped across her shoulders to dangle before her face. The ends tickled the tops of her breasts, but her mind could not focus on that. Not with his hands still circling and now his mouth pressed to the base of her neck.

She frowned. Without her realizing it, he had slipped out of her grasp. He now stood above her and her hand rested again on his taut thigh.

"I want to touch you," she said as she tightened her grip on his leg.

"You are touching me, and I am touching you. Do you feel my dragon stroking you?"

She shook her head, and her hair brushed across the backs of his hands before dropping on top of her nipples.

"Close your eyes and listen closer. You will feel it."

She did, trying to hear over the rapid beat of her heart. She felt a presence inside her. An energy that throbbed and tingled deep in her core. Was that him? Rubbing against her womb? That was what it felt like—a thick, wonderful presence deep in her belly. Not physical, and yet she felt it so clearly.

And while she was focused so intently on the sensations in her belly, he bit the back of her neck. She gasped, arching in reaction. "Is that your dragon power? That…" She gasped again as the energy deep in her belly shifted—seeming to slide up and down inside her. "Oh, God."

He didn't answer except to swirl his tongue over the bite on her neck. Her entire body was trembling. It was wonderful and terrifying at the same time. She had never even imagined sex like this.

"Don't think," he said against her spine. His mouth had dropped lower now to just below the base of her neck. "Just feel."

She didn't have a choice as he nipped then soothed the nobs of her spine. Her shoulders trembled. Then he dropped another inch. She felt his lips tickling her skin, murmuring something against her secret vulnerability—the spot high between her shoulder blades. It was her secret vice and the reason she kept her hair long. She loved the feel of something touching her at the center point between her shoulders.

He knew about it. He knew how to brush his lips ever so lightly right there. No bites—that would be too much—but then he did something that made all the strength go out of her legs. He flattened his mouth against her skin and sucked. Once, lightly. Then again, harder. And then a third time—hard.

*Pop!* It felt as if he'd popped a cork, and out of the hole poured energy. It was a simple stream at first, tingling as it passed through her spine and into him. But then far below in her belly, his energy stroke thrust hard, pulsing in time with the suction of his mouth. It was a like a pump, pushing the power flow upward.

His hands began to move on her breasts, as well. He squeezed her nipples rhythmically—everything was timed together—adding power and strength to the river of current flowing through her.

Then her orgasm began. It wasn't a ripple as she was used to on those secret nights alone. This was a full-body explosion that began with her womb, bringing her thighs along as she squeezed her legs together. Her entire lower body began to pulse in time with the compression of her nipples. She undulated from bottom to top where he pulled the power out with his mouth.

The contractions increased. More and yet more. She didn't even have the breath to scream. He changed his grip on her nipples, pulling now instead of squeezing. She might have been horrified, but what it did to her breasts added to the power. Every stroke sent tiny fire bolts from her breasts to her core, adding to the orgasmic wave— there was no other way to describe it—that rolled up her spine. And it was still building.

Oh, God. Her fingers were throbbing. Her hair was on end. Even her brain was orgasming. And still it went on. She thought she was going to pass out from the pleasure of it all. Nobody could withstand this forever. She was going to have a brain aneurism or something.

Oceanic waves of pleasure crashed up her spine. More and more. She heard him gasp and the suction broke against her skin. It was just a moment until his lips returned, but it was enough to disrupt the rhythm. The internal pump continued, but his hands were no longer steady. He was shuddering!

She felt his tongue, swirling again at that wonderful place, and she felt the flow increase again, but not for long. The overall response was diminishing.

"No…" she whispered. And yet there was welcome relief, as well. A steady glow was replacing the waves, which were steadying into a sweet tremble. She was able to take a breath, and for a moment the increased oxygen added a surge to the contractions. But all too soon that faded. The current continued, tightening from a river down to a stream into a tiny thin wire still vibrating up her spine to his lips. How bright she felt! Like a wire filament in a lightbulb burning brighter than the sun. Then it, too, began to dim. A thousand watts. A hundred watts. A simple night-light of gentle warmth.

She collapsed forward, completely boneless. He took her weight easily. She barely noticed when he shifted her to lie sideways in his arms. Then without another word, he lifted her up and carried her from the kitchen.

She drifted in and out of consciousness as he climbed the stairs. It wasn't that she lost herself into darkness. Her entire body still glowed. She simply lost awareness of the world as she floated in a bright sea of joy.

He set her down in her bed and stripped her out of her sweatpants with quick efficient movements. He left her panties on, though she would have preferred he take those, too. His hands were respectful, even reverent, as if what he did was a form of worship.

Tracy wanted to say something, but she didn't know what. She wanted to thank him or hold him or ask when they could do that again, but she hadn't the control. Instead, she let him pull the covers over her nearly naked body then brush the hair from her face.

The stroke of his fingertips across her cheek revived the fireflies for a brief second. They tingled in his wake, then quieted back into satiated ecstasy. She felt his lips then, a brief touch on her mouth followed by a long slow stroke of his tongue across her lower lip. It was the coup de grâce, and she roused herself enough to open her eyes when he pulled away.

"That…" She didn't know what to say. It had been overwhelmingly incredible? Beyond imagination fabulous? Nothing fit, and she saw his lips curve in a very male smugness.

"That was just the beginning," he said. "You are in balance for now. Yin and yang are equalized and so your body will be able to rest. Find me tomorrow if you want to learn more."

# 7

THE KNOCK ON HIS DOOR was insistent. A rapid three beats—bap, bap, bap—then a pause only to begin again. Bap, bap, bap. Loud enough to be heard, but not loud enough to disturb the neighbors at… Nathan glanced at his cell phone—2:17 a.m.

He knew who it was. Tracy. No one else would disturb him at this hour. But it was eight days since their last encounter. He'd given up hope that his landlady would return.

He shoved out of bed, pulling on his teaching pants merely because they were the closest thing at hand. His toes curled in reaction as they touched the chilled wood floor, but that was all to the good. His dragon had leaped fully awake at the Tracy's first knock. Now that she was on her fourth series of taps, freezing feet could only help him walk upright.

"I'm coming," he grumbled, annoyed to realize how strong his voice was and how quickly he made it to the door. Given the power of her yin energy, he had expected her to show up a week ago. After two days of waiting, he had begun to worry. Had she hurt herself? She hadn't been around the apartment building at all. One of his neighbor's walls remained half-painted and the front hallway had grown cluttered with fall leaves and muddy footprints.

After five days absence, he realized what must have happened. A tigress's awakening was unusual among students who'd trained for years and Tracy was a neophyte. So when he'd pulled all that yin from her in her kitchen, her feminine aspect must have gone back to sleep. With her yin and yang balanced, she had returned to her normal life, probably working hard to forget it had ever happened. And since she was likely embarrassed by the events, she would avoid him like the plague, and he would never see her again.

The pain of that thought had left him unable to study for two more days. Tonight had been the first night he had managed to fall into an exhausted sleep despite the woman who still haunted his thoughts. And now here she was, hovering uncertainly on the other side of his door in the middle of the night. Could he have been wrong? Was her tigress still awake? If so, a week's loss of training would have built up the yin in her system to a frightening level. And wouldn't that just serve her right for ignoring him—and her own condition—for over a week?

He was grinning as he unlocked the door, but he pretended sleepiness. He cracked the entrance wide enough to see her clearly, but not enough to invite her in. Then he leaned against the door frame and prepared to look his fill at his gorgeous landlady.

The smile faded the moment he saw her. She looked wonderful and terrible at the same time. Her eyes were bright and clear, but with a feverish intensity that seemed to eat him alive. She wore baggy sweats and a loose T-shirt, but her body clearly reacted to every shift of the ugly fabric. Her nipples were pointed; her hips swayed in enticement, even as she folded her arms across her chest and swallowed in anxiety.

Her tigress was still awake. And clearly, she had tried to deny it, suppressing the demands of her awakened body until she was literally sick with her own yin abundance.

"Sorry to wake you, Mr. Gao," she said. Her voice held a husky rasp that went straight to his organ, tightening his dragon pearls to painful intensity.

He didn't answer. He didn't trust himself. Everything inside him urged that he drag her inside his apartment and relieve her suffering. But he'd already done that a week ago. He'd balanced her chi in a night that still haunted his thoughts. She needed training, not a quick fix.

"May I come in?" she asked.

He took a deep breath and immediately regretted it. She was surrounded by the musky smell of a tigress on the prowl. It burrowed deep into a man, bypassing his mind and going straight for the most primal needs.

"I…I need to come in, Mr. Gao. Nathan. Please."

"You need to balance your energy again, Miss Williams. You have let things go way too long."

She swallowed, her skin becoming even more pale. "That's…um…what I wanted to talk to you about." She glanced nervously about the empty hallway. "Can I come in please?"

"Why?"

She ran a hand through her full, shimmering hair. His dragon reacted predictably to the sight of the wavy brown silk. His mind saw that her hand trembled. "I thought…I mean, I hoped… I would like to see if you would." She closed her eyes, then said something that must have cost her greatly in pride. "I brought condoms. A whole box."

His dragon leaped forward. She noticed, of course. His loose pants could not hide everything. She stepped forward, sure of her welcome, but he didn't move. Though lust rode him hard, he resolutely barred the door to her.

"You don't need another balancing, Miss Williams. You need training."

"Okay. Okay." She put her hand on the door. "But I can't think right now."

He didn't budge. "What have you been doing? Ignoring it? Hoping it would go away?"

She flushed. The rosy tint to her cheeks looked better than any model's and then she wet her lips, leaving behind a glossy shimmer that nearly made him miss her next words.

"I thought maybe it was just one of those things, you know?"

He did know. But he couldn't let her give in to the need to just forget. "And now?"

She looked up and tears shimmered in her eyes. "I've been having these thoughts. Lustful thoughts. Fantasies." Her voice dropped to a husky whisper. "Urges."

"A tigress must be satisfied. That's why—"

"About my brother's friends!" she continued, her voice tight with panic. "Boys! Young, teenage boys in their football gear with their tight bottoms lifting up." She swallowed. "I was watching a game and you don't want to know what I was thinking!"

He could well imagine. But she didn't stop long enough for him to comment.

"I touched one of them. Not on purpose. Well, yes on purpose, but not because I meant to. I mean…" She closed her eyes.

"Did you hurt him?"

"What? No! I was working concessions and he came for a drink. A bottled purple…whatever. I took his money.

I got his bottle. But when I was handing it over…" Her voice broke. "He wasn't even cute, but it didn't matter. He was young and healthy and when I touched his hand, I looked into his eyes." She raised her gaze, humiliation staining her cheeks. "I licked my lips and smiled. It wasn't anything, except it was. He knew what I meant. I knew what I meant. Thank God there were other people there. Part of me was ready to take him behind the bleachers right then and there!"

He frowned, not understanding her panic. "But you did nothing wrong."

"But I wanted to! Don't you see? He was my brother's friend!" Her voice was rising on a wail of panic that would soon alert his neighbors. And then she startled him. She shoved hard against the doorway, her hunger overcoming her natural restraint. "Please let me in, Nathan."

He stared at her, his thoughts whirling in confusion. He had grown up in a tigress temple, seen women learning the ways of sexuality from the moment he could focus his vision. His own dragon education had begun when he was just learning to read; in fact, his first Chinese characters had been learned from the sacred texts. Never, ever had he met a woman so stubbornly confused by her own sexuality. And that, heaven help him, was in part why she was so attractive to him.

Every woman at the temple had tried to seduce him or his brother at one time or another. They were the only men around. But Nathan had never felt such an incredible pull toward any of them. Tracy was the exact opposite of every woman he'd ever known. She was competent at business, strong physically, and not in the least bit averse to hard work. And yet on the sexual side, she was nervous and uncertain. Before all this had begun, she'd been a shy flirt. And now, she resisted her sexuality until she was literally sick with it. Who could understand such a woman? And who could resist teaching her to embrace her feminine power?

"Nathan," she whispered, her voice making his belly tighten with hunger. "Please. I don't want them. I want you."

"Why did you wait?" he pressed.

"I…I…" She swallowed, then she looked into his eyes and he saw stark terror in them. "I'm afraid. I don't want to do this. I don't want to be like this."

"But why?" He truly didn't understand. What woman wouldn't want to be a sexual goddess? A woman lusted after by every man alive?

"Just make it go away. Make it all stop."

"You have to come to a class, Tracy. You have to learn to control the tigress." The need to comfort her burned inside. He wanted to hold her, to take the fear from her eyes. But if he touched her, if he once gave in to temptation, there would be no stopping. He was already rock hard, his every cell straining for her. "I cannot take advantage of you like this," he said, as much to himself as to her.

"I'll pay you."

He blinked, her words dousing his fire more effectively than a cold shower. "I'm sorry?"

She blanched, then abruptly rubbed her hand over her face. "I don't know what I'm saying. Nathan, I don't know what to do!"

God help him, he was tempted. She obviously needed help. She didn't yet realize that she would need balancing on a regular basis. Weekly, at least. It was not as if it were a hardship for him, but he couldn't do it. He couldn't use her like that even though every cell in his body screamed for him to ease her suffering.

Nathan moved fast. Spinning around, he grabbed a book off his shelf, then returned to the door to block it before she could push her way in. He nearly didn't make it. She had her shoulder against the door, but he caught it before she could nudge it open. He shoved the book at her, careful not to touch her or his resistance would crumple entirely.

"Study this," he said. "It will give you basic exercises. Don't come back until you have mastered the initial forms."

She stared at him, her mouth slipping open in shock. "You want me to read a book?" she gasped. "When you could… When we could be… You want me to read?"

*No!* "Yes."

Her eyes widened as the truth finally hit her. He wasn't going to touch her tonight. "But there's another football game tomorrow evening!"

He tried not to imagine it. He tried not to think of her under the bleachers with any one of the willing American boys who would happily join her there. "Read fast," he said. And then he did the hardest thing he'd ever done in his entire life.

He shut the door.

# 8

TRACY WAS SITTING by his door when he returned from class the next day. Her body still radiated beauty, but her shoulders were slumped with defeat.

He knelt down before her, his sympathy fully engaged. "You could have used your pass key."

She frowned. "I wouldn't violate your privacy that way."

Progress. "Why are you here, Tracy?"

"I went to a bar."

His breath stopped and his mind reeled. She didn't look hurt, but anything could have happened. The dangers—

"I thought if you wouldn't help, then someone else would."

"Tracy," he whispered, unable to say more. But a wealth of anguish vibrated through her name. She must have heard it because her gaze jumped to his.

"I couldn't do it, Nathan. If my vibrator wasn't doing what I needed, then meaningless sex with a stranger wouldn't, either." She shuddered then she looked him straight in the eye. "I want you. I've wanted you for months."

His breath froze in his chest. What had happened to his shy landlord? The one who flirted so sweetly, but never went beyond the initial stages? He knew the answer. He knew and he mourned. "You're a tigress, Tracy. You want to train, to go to the temple and eventually to walk with divine angels. You don't actually want me." He swallowed.

It killed him to say it, but he had to remind himself that it was the truth. She was a tigress. She was destined for bigger things than him. And no matter how much she thought she wanted him right now, he was only one step on the path. Hadn't he experienced exactly that dozens of times? How many tigresses had sworn they wanted only him? Then once their needs had been met, they'd moved on to the next man. It was what tigresses did. They craved yang power from as many men as possible as often as possible.

As long as he remembered that, then he could teach Tracy and send her to the temple. Sighing, he cupped her elbow. "Come inside."

She nodded, already straightening. "I want to learn, Nathan. I'll do whatever it takes." Then she flashed him a wry smile. "But it's gotta be fast. There's another football game in a few hours."

"Enlightenment doesn't have a schedule, you know."

She grinned, and for the first time in a long while, he saw hope sparkle in her eyes. "I have faith in you."

He didn't answer. As a teacher, he knew he should remind her that her faith should be placed in herself, but Nathan couldn't quite say the words. He liked her reliance on him. He wanted to be the one to show her the path to Truth. And so he opened his apartment door to her.

"I read your book," she said as he locked the door behind her. "I tried the exercises, but…"

He waited, arching an eyebrow when she flushed and ducked her head.

"I'm not very flexible."

No, she was strong and muscular. The renovations she had done on the building had given her a toned body sculpted for work, not femininity. And yet when he looked at her, her beauty still grabbed him deep in his gut.

"You will learn." He shucked his jacket, then arranged a set of cushions on the floor. "Please sit. Tell me what you did and how it felt."

She folded herself awkwardly onto the cushions, obviously self-conscious. "I…uh…I did the breast exercises. It felt…" She shrugged. "Useless. It wasn't anything like what we did before. You know, in my kitchen."

He remembered. He'd relived it a thousand times in his fantasies. "You felt nothing?"

"Nada." She sighed. "I'm not even sure I believe in this stuff."

He looked at her. Why was she so stubborn?

"I mean, I do," she said in a rush. "Something sure as hell is wrong with me, but—"

"You are not wrong!" he snapped. "You have awakened as a woman. Why do you fight it?"

She reared back, stunned by his fury. Truthfully, he was a little startled himself. She bit her lip and looked down at her hands. "I'm sorry," she finally said. "I haven't even asked how your day was."

He blinked, completely thrown. "I'm sorry?"

Tracy smiled, the curve of her mouth softening her face. "Let's itemize our relationship so far, shall we? There was a wonderful couple months of almost conversations in the hallway. Then I accuse you of illegal activity and try to throw you out of my building. Then I come to a class, run out screaming, only to have you follow and give me the most fabulous night of my life."

"I cannot claim credit for—"

"Don't interrupt, Mr. Gao. Then I ignore you for over a week only to show up in the middle of the night, try to buy you, and now I'm stalking you." She leaned forward. "Is this the usual path to enlightenment?"

He smiled. "Nothing with you is usual, Miss Williams."

"So, answer my question—how was your day?"

He shook his head, wondering where to begin. "My mother is spending too much money again, or so my sister said in her e-mail. I am cold in your Illinois November. And my classes are hard. I understand the material, but my English is not fast enough sometimes. Everything takes longer for me."

"I can't even imagine trying to study in a foreign language. I nearly failed Spanish in high school." She shifted to sit cross-legged. She was not aware of how the simple act of opening her legs like that focused his gaze. "So why do it?" she asked. "Aren't there schools in Hong Kong?"

He nodded, forcing himself to look back to her face. "This university is one of the best in the world for business. When I am finished, I will have my choice of jobs."

"You aiming for a big industry career?" There was a note of surprise in her voice, but his eyes were held by the curve of her lips, the shift of her mouth. "Nathan?"

He blinked. "I…uh…I aim for a big career."

She smiled. She had the most perfectly colored lips— soft rose that deepened to red when she grew excited. "I understand that," she said. "Big career. Big money. That's what I want, too." Then she looked about his apartment, her gaze taking in his poor clothing and sparse furnishings. "I just wouldn't have guessed you as the power-and-fame type."

He followed her gaze, seeing no privation. He had the luxury of a whole room to himself with no spying eyes, no critical gazes, no demanding students. "I am happy with very little," he said honestly. "But the temple requires a great deal of money to support it. And I have siblings who want to do as I do—go to school, advance, have a future beyond temple drudgery. If I do not make good, my whole family could starve."

She frowned, obviously startled. "You're exaggerating, right? They're not actually starving, are they?"

He looked down. How did he explain the realities of the Hong Kong poor? "We live on an outlying island. It took an hour and a half for my sister to ferry then bus to school. She would leave at four in the morning so that she could meet other students at the library and tutor them for money. A few years ago, she gave it up as too difficult, but I know she longs for more. My brother, too. They both want more education, more opportunity but there is no money for it."

She shifted to her knees, and he saw her breasts bounce. Her nipples were already hard, and they drew his gaze. "What about your parents?"

"My mother and her sister run the tigress temple. Like all tigresses, their hearts and minds are devoted to ascension to the immortal realm. They take in students for money, but there are many mouths to feed."

"How many?"

He shrugged as he settled down beside her. A teacher should not sit this close to the student, but he couldn't resist. He wanted to be near her. "Twenty students live with us, plus my brother and sister. My aunt."

"And your father?"

Nathan leaned closer, letting the sweetness of her scent add spice to his thoughts. "I function as father. I am the eldest male. It is my responsibility to see that all are cared for."

She frowned. "But that's a couple dozen people. Surely they can work. They can do something."

He tilted his head, wondering at her surprise. "I am the eldest male," he answered simply.

And when she still didn't seem to follow, he pushed to his feet. This closeness to her interfered with his thoughts. He wasn't thinking before speaking. And now he was trying to explain the realities of a Chinese family to an American woman. She couldn't possibly understand, and yet he still continued. "It's a temple. We have a garden for vegetables and some farm animals, but no money for repairs, for texts, for all the things that a large group of people need."

"That's a lot of maintenance," she said. "How old is the building?"

"Three buildings. The temple has stood for more than a hundred years."

She released a whistle, low in her throat. It was not a sexual sound, and yet his dragon responded as if it were a siren call. "Like I said, a lot of maintenance." She shook her head. "But you're only one person. You can't possibly support them all."

He shrugged. "I am the eldest male."

"Yeah, I got that. Isn't that a little sexist? I mean, to take that all on yourself because—"

"Don't you care for your brother? Did you hesitate when your parents died?"

She leaned back. "Of course, I took care of him. He's all I've got. But he's just one person, and we're barely scraping by. If it weren't for the insurance money, we'd have lost everything. I still worry that social services is going to show up and take him away."

He looked at her, guessing at the strength required to keep both her and Joey together. "You must have been very young. Barely eighteen."

She shrugged. "It didn't matter. He was my family. I'd do anything for him."

He remained silent, wondering if she would see that he did nothing more than she did. He was holding his family together. Even from a continent apart, he would see that they survived.

It took her a moment, but in the end, her eyes widened in shock. "You can't seriously expect to support two dozen people."

"I can, and I will." He straightened, showing her a dragon's determination in every line of his body. "But I must get my education. That is why the temple goes even longer without electricity."

She studied him, but he could not read her face. Did she understand what he was trying to do? Could she comprehend the drive to succeed—not for himself, but for all who depended on him?

She pushed to her feet. Her motions were smooth and infinitely feminine. Then she touched him—a gentle hand laid on his shoulders. He felt the warmth of her body all the way through to his soul. "I had no idea," she whispered. "I can't even imagine. The pressure must be incredible."

He shook his head. "I have borne the responsibility since my earliest days."

"I can see that," she said softly, admiration in her tone. "But isn't it hard? I mean, desperately, horribly hard?

Don't you long for something more, something beyond the everyday drudgery?"

He should step away from her. The feel of her hand was drugging him. It brought out fantasies that leeched all the blood from his brain. But he could not force himself to break the connection. Instead, he wrapped his hand around hers and brought it to his lips. "It is my dream to support my family," he said. He wanted to kiss her, but that was one of the most cardinal rules between teacher and student: no kisses, no touching except to demonstrate. And no sexual relations whatsoever.

"Nathan…" she murmured. Her face was flushed, her breath coming in short, quick pants. Her inner tigress was riding her hard. He had to stop this.

He dropped his forehead against hers, allowing himself the connection while keeping his distance from her lips. "What is your dream?" he asked. "What do you yearn for?"

She shuddered. He guessed that the tigress inside her fought the restraint of simple conversation. But she was not a woman to give in to simple lust. "See, that's the thing, Nathan. Everybody else has dreams, but I…I just want money. We've got the basics, but a cushion would make me breathe so much easier."

Her scent pervaded his mind. It rose from her skin and fogged his senses. "But there are many ways to make money," he said. "How will you—"

"Stockbroker," she answered, the word rushed out and breathless. "It's all about hard work with them. The harder they work, the more they get. And I plan to work very, very hard."

He had no doubt about that. How sad that her dream and her fortune would never come about. Whether she understood it or not, the tigress in her would override her mundane desires. In time, the quest for immortality would become paramount. She would leave everything she knew to train at the temple. It wasn't what she wanted. It certainly wasn't what Nathan wanted for her. But he had seen it happen too many times. Spirit would choose. Her mind and body would have no choice but to follow.

"What about you?" she asked, her voice a low rasp that further fogged his mind. He knew that a relationship between them was doomed to disaster, and yet she called to him on so many levels. Her body was the least of her lures. She was focused on the same things he was: supporting a family and trying to create a better life for them. And she was kind, trying to talk to him as a person and not as a tool. Those two things alone were so rare in his life. He could not think of another soul—save maybe his sister—who acted in such a way.

"Nathan?" she pressed, clearly wondering about his silence. "I'm sorry. Have I come at a bad time? You're probably really busy—"

"And if I am?" he pressed, wondering exactly how generous she was. "Would you leave me alone now? What about the football game tonight?"

Tracy bit her lip, her anxiety obvious. "I won't go. I'll lock myself in my room and study the book you gave me."

"It won't be enough," he said. "You need a teacher."

She licked her lips, and his dragon reared. "I won't be ruled by this." She lifted up enough to look him in the eye. "I want to be a woman, I want to explore my sexuality, but I won't let it control me."

She meant it. But she had no idea how strong the desire could grow. "Most tigresses aren't so interested in controlling themselves as much as controlling other people. Other men."

She pulled back, obviously repulsed by the concept. "I don't think I like your tigresses very much."

He shrugged. "A tigress is pursued by all men. It is important that she learn how to protect herself."

"That's not a very good excuse. Control comes from within. And only over ourselves."

He smiled, his heart and his body fully caught now. "You might very well be the salvation of our temple."

She released a self-conscious laugh. "I just want to be able to go to a football game without losing my mind."

"Then we should begin," he said. He didn't really mean it. He just wanted to touch her. Unable to stop himself, he stroked the soft skin of her cheek. She closed her eyes, lifting her face to his touch.

"Is this what you did at the temple?" she asked. "Did you teach a lot of girls?"

"No," he said, his face already dropping closer. His mouth was almost on hers. "I used to teach, but then my talents were needed elsewhere."

She shifted her head so that his fingers brushed across her lips. "Doing what?"

"The accounts. I cashed the checks for classes and paid the bills. I decided on the repairs and on the luxuries."

"You made things run smoothly," she said. "How old were you when you started doing that?"

"From the moment I could read," he answered.

She stopped rubbing her lips across his finger. "Wow. I started at eighteen, and it sucked then. You must have been a baby. I can't even imagine how hard it was for you."

She understood. Nathan could see it in her eyes, and it

made his breath catch in his throat. She understood more than his own mother what he had done as a boy, and how hard he'd worked to bring order to a very chaotic world.

"Do you miss it?" she continued. "Do you long to go back to Hong Kong?"

"No. I miss my brother and sister. I will make sure that they have everything they want. But no, I will never go back to that life."

Her eyes widened in surprise. "Never? Was it so very bad?"

He shook his head, refusing to elaborate. How could he explain a house of two dozen beautiful, sexual women intent on seducing him while completely ignoring the mundane realities of life? Not a one understood bills or plumbing or even the basics of preparing a meal because their minds were completely absorbed with their sexuality. And his mother was the worst of the lot. As a child, he'd had to learn quickly about fixing his own food or starve.

There were a few who had helped. Tigress cubs too early in their training to have tasted the glories of heaven, too new to have lost all earthly focus yet. They helped him when they could, guided him as a mother or a lover.

But then came that first touch of divinity, that first moment of true ecstasy and all was forgotten—their promises to him, their whispered love, even simple kindnesses were lost in the search for heaven.

That was what it meant to be a tigress, and he would not subject himself to it anymore. In fact, his whole focus was to earn enough money so that his brother and sister could escape, as well. Falling in love with yet another tigress cub was not in the realm of possibility for him. He could not do it. He would not.

And yet, Tracy did not act like any tigress he knew. Tracy had not lost herself in the quest for immortality yet. And Tracy understood him as no one else had ever bothered to try. He knew eventually the spirit would take her. She would taste ecstasy and he would be abandoned once again. Nathan knew, but he couldn't stop himself.

He kissed her. He claimed her mouth the way a dragon would claim a woman. He took her; he ate her alive, and he relished every second of her surrender.

# 9

SHE HAD BEEN WAITING AGES for his kiss. She had dreamed of this moment, hungered desperately for it. And it had been worth the wait.

A week ago, they had been strangers in an incredible night of passion. Now they were friends. When he leaned in to kiss her, her entire body stretched for his lips. She met his mouth with a yearning that had nothing to do with his strange tigress rites. It wasn't hunger that drove her, but a warmth of shared secrets.

But passion wasn't far behind. Lightning burned through her system, beginning with where their lips touched and searing through her senses. She came alive in an instant. She opened her mouth wide, seeking to devour him, but he was there before her.

His arm wrapped around her waist, gripping her tightly to him. His mouth slanted over hers and his tongue thrust into her. She matched him in intensity, but not in skill. He knew just how to excite her. His tongue teased then pushed, toyed then thrust. In and out while she tried to keep up. In the end, she gave herself up to the experience. No, she gave herself to him. It was time for her to become a woman in all senses, and she wanted to do it with him.

Tracy burrowed her hands into his silky black hair and

arched into his embrace. When he broke off the kiss to breathe, she dropped her head against his shoulder and trembled from the force of their desire.

"This isn't practice," he said. "I'm not being a teacher. Teachers don't kiss. Teachers don't—"

She pulled his head back to her mouth. She didn't want an instructor—she wanted a man. She wanted him. "Tell me what to do," she said against his lips. "Tell me what you want."

"Let me open your yin gates," he said, already pushing her down onto the floor.

She went willingly, gripping his broad shoulders for balance. "What can I do for you? What—"

He hovered over her, his dark eyes piercing even in shadow. "I want to drink you up. I need to feel you surround me. Please." His hands coiled under her shirt, trembling over her bare belly but not pushing higher.

"Yes," she answered, not even knowing what he wanted.

He pulled off her loose T-shirt in one quick movement. She helped as best she could, raising her arms so that the fabric could fly free. And while her hands were still in the air, he popped the clasp on her bra.

"You've done this before," she commented drily.

Nathan shook his head. "Not like this. Not as a man."

She smiled, unaccountably pleased by his words. She lay down now, her upper body completely exposed to him. He looked at her for a long moment, his right hand hovering ever so tentatively over her belly, then higher to shape the air above her left breast.

"You are a water soul," he said as he looked at her. "Your body is full and round."

"Is that your way of saying I'm fat?"

He glanced startled at her face. "No. It means whenever I see you, I think of full mountain streams, of glorious oceans. Your body nourishes whatever you touch, you give life to the world."

He saw her as some sort of water goddess, lush and full? Tracy touched his face to reassure herself that he was real. That this stunningly beautiful man was looking at her as if she were the answer to his prayers. His skin burned fever hot beneath her fingers, and she tugged at his dress shirt. "Take it off," she urged.

He did, though his hands fumbled with the buttons. He hadn't even stripped it fully off before his mouth descended to her breast. He began with tiny bites in the skin around the areola that had her toes curling in delight. And just like in her kitchen, a power began to build inside her chest. "My breasts feel like they're ten times larger than before. It's like there's something there, trying to break free."

"It is your yin power. Your breasts are the lesser yin gates." He leaned down, pressing a long, tender kiss at the shallow spot between each breast. "I can open it, Tracy. I want to open it, but it will be intense."

More intense than this? She almost giggled at the thought. But then she realized he was serious. "More than that first night at my house? I mean, this feels similar…."

He lifted up. "I pulled your energy out last time. This will be different. I will open the gates to your breasts first, then move lower down to your cinnabar cave."

This time she did laugh. "My what?"

His hands dropped to the clasp of her jeans, toying with the rivet there. "If they are both open, a circle flow can begin. Drawing in from below, pumping up to your breasts, and then back down."

"Like before?"

He nodded. "But better. Stronger." He flashed her a grin. "I will be bathed in your power and you will scream."

She felt her lips curl in a slow smile. "A good scream?"

He grinned. "A very good scream. And it will last for a long, long time." Then he paused. "But think carefully, Tracy. Once I do this, you can never go back. Your tigress will be fully released. There will be no—"

"I don't want to go back to sleep. I don't want it gone." She gripped his shoulders, pulling herself up to kiss him with all the hunger inside her. He opened himself to her demand, meeting her tongue with his own powerful thrust. Then he eased her back down onto the cushion.

"You must remove your jeans, Tracy. Know that you choose this."

He was trying to make her hesitate, to think of the consequences of her actions. She didn't need to doubt herself. She knew what she wanted. She stripped with quick motions. And when she lay naked before him, she looked him in the eyes.

"This is what I want," she said clearly. "And I want you to do it." Did he understand? Did he know that she trusted him and no other? There wasn't time to explain.

At her words, his nostrils flared. His hands came to her chest, but then stopped and hovered just above her skin. "Close your eyes. I want you to feel every second of what is to come."

She shook her head. "I want to see you."

He arched a single sculpted brow in surprise. "So be it." And with that he began to touch her breasts. She felt a fine tremor in his caress, a vibration in his fingers that told her he was not nearly as confident as he seemed. But then thought faded beneath other sensations. He was a master at this. He began with simple strokes, shaping her breasts into a fine point, then tweaking the nipples at unexpected moments. Her body became a pulsing wave of sensation, and yet her mind remained clear. While she gasped and trembled beneath his strokes, she watched his face, his eyes.

He was fully absorbed in what he did. His attention focused entirely on her pleasure. This was more than sex to him. He believed it was a spiritual awakening. Sex your way to heaven. It was ridiculous, and yet the more he caressed her, the more she felt a power building. Not orgasm, though she was certainly headed in that direction. This was more.

"Look at me," she gasped.

He did, his hands slowing only the tiniest bit. "Tracy?"

"What does this mean?"

He frowned. "I am opening—"

"To you, Nathan. What does this mean to you?" Was this just sex to him?

She could tell he didn't understand her question. And in truth, she wasn't sure she wanted an honest answer. Much better to simply close her eyes and enjoy what he gave her. And yet she kept her eyes stubbornly open.

"I am helping you reach your full potential." He smiled. "Are you ready?"

She nodded. A lie. She had no idea if she was ready or not. But his smile reassured her. He cupped each breast, shaping them such that the nipples stretched toward him. Then he began to squeeze—not painfully, but in a rhythm that her body quickly began to echo. Then he leaned down to suck on one breast. A light kiss, then a stronger nip.

Then a long hard pull that had her arching up, her breath caught in her throat. It felt as if he were pulling on a cord, one that connected her breast to her brain and her womb. And each pull on that cord arched through her like a bow, drawing the power inside her tighter, stronger and more focused at the point where his mouth licked her nipple.

Then he moved to the other breast and repeated the process. Kiss. Nip. Pull. Back and forth he went between breasts, keeping the rhythm steady. And with each sequence, the power inside her became more focused, more insistent.

At the beginning, her legs had been slack, her knees lightly touching. Now they spread of their own accord, her heels digging into the floor, her hips undulating with his rhythm. Her breath came in gasps, timed with him. And her breasts… They were the focus of everything. Tingling fireflies, horny lightning, all of that was nothing to what she felt now. Her body was her breasts, and they were huge with energy—throbbing, sizzling, aching.

He was concentrating on her left breast. The kiss. The nip. Those were the same as before—wonderful, but not enough. And then the pull. Hard. Sharp. Just like before, only this time something new happened. Another hard pull. Another *pop!* Like a plug pulling free, and a burning current of energy gushed forth. She had to look down to see that she wasn't actually on fire. It wasn't visible, but the sensations were real. Her left arm spasmed with the fire, but he didn't stop. He quickly focused on her other breast.

No sequence this time. Just the pull. Again and again. While her entire left side felt as if it were pouring lava, born from deep within her. And then, *pop!* The other side began its own current.

"There is so much," Nathan gasped from above her. She couldn't speak. White light was searing through her brain as her entire chest seemed to open up. Her back was arched from the power of what he had released.

Then she felt him between her legs. The sensations all blurred together, but his mouth was cool and wet where she throbbed. He supported her hips with his arms, though he barely needed to. He kissed her, then swirled his tongue through all the right places. Then he did a long, sucking pull. Oh, my God. Kiss. Swirl. Pull. Kiss. Swirl. Pull.

The orgasm came in a rush—but there were so many other sensations that she almost didn't notice. The contractions deep in her belly were a simple addition to the steady rhythm he had started with. But now her entire spine was involved, contracting below, pushing the energy upward, where it swirled at her chest before dispersing.

He began lifting and lowering her hips. An inch down, an inch up. He timed each beat with the same sequence— kiss, swirl, pull. She hadn't known it was possible to orgasm for more than a few seconds, but now she realized that with every beat, the contractions intensified.

"Too much," she gasped. Much too much. Her entire body was beginning to undulate as her contractions still gained in strength. Her toes were curling, drawing power up her shins and thighs. Then his mouth added to the pulse and the power. Her belly contracted, pushing the energy higher.

Her head was thrown back, then her neck began to throb with what he did. She arched then released then arched again. Her fingers clutched the cushions, contracting of their own accord at his rhythm. Her arms added their power, as did her breath, her thoughts, her entire being.

All collected—collided—beneath her breast bone where flash after flash of energy burst through her breasts. It was all energy—invisible but so real—and it was coalescing into a river that poured out of her.

And still he continued. He was gripping her hips now, otherwise she would have bucked out of his hands. Kiss. Swirl. Pull. "Open!" he cried, the order adding its own vibration to the overwhelming pulse. "Open now!"

Then he put his mouth on her and sucked sharply. Whoosh! The energy door flew open right below his lips. Only this point did not release power, it drew it in. She felt the roar of lightning spear through her. From clit to womb it burst in, then remained—a steadily growing current of fire—moving inward. Upward. And her orgasm that had been strong before, now grew in proportion and intensity.

"Do you feel the circle?" he asked. "Does the power flow from breast to womb and back up?"

It did. She could feel it. Her orgasm pumped the heat up her spine until the energy flowed from her chest. But now, it continued outside her body, then curled back in, drawing up that bright cord from clit to womb, adding more velocity to the flow, more current. More power.

An eternal feedback loop of fire. It grew and grew until she felt pierced by a river of light. Expanding through her groin, widening through her belly as the orgasmic pump pushed the energy upward again.

She began to scream. It wasn't a single cry, but an ever-expanding sound that engulfed her. She was no longer a body encasing a river. She became the river. Her body was simply a small part—the smallest part—of an ever-growing circle of sensation.

Her mind shut down. She was a river of joy. She was beyond anything she had ever known.

Ecstasy.

NATHAN GENTLY SETTLED Tracy on his bed, taking time to cover her though her body still burned with yin fire. He didn't even have to touch her to feel her heat. She radiated like the sun and he closed his eyes for a moment just to appreciate it.

Her yin power washed over him, warm and sensuous but with the strength that was integral to her character. He took a deep breath. And then another. And in the third, clarity flashed through his mind.

It was happening again. The forbidden event, and the real reason he had chosen to go to school in the United States. He was falling in love with a student. Attachments were inevitable between teacher and pupil, but this was more. When he saw Tracy, he didn't just take pride in her progress, in the shift from skeptic to tigress. He saw the fierce love she poured into this building and the softening in her eyes when she spoke about her brother. She was a tigress in more ways than her sexuality. And he was falling hard for her.

He sighed and forced himself to step away. She was a tigress. She belonged at the temple. And he… He had no wish to go back there again. His life was ahead of him, not back in Hong Kong with greedy tigresses.

Though it tore at his soul to admit it, he could no longer stay around Tracy. He had to end their relationship now before he lost himself in her. He would not fall in love with Tracy.

He booted up his laptop and began composing an

e-mail to the Tigress Mother and the head male practitioner Dragon Stephen Chu. With the right words, he could ensure that Tracy had a place at the temple. Even more, he knew that after a few choice hints, Stephen would move heaven and earth to get this newest tigress beside him in Hong Kong.

Within a week, Tracy would probably be half a world away.

# 10

TRACY WOKE ON A LUMPY mattress to the sound of…horse racing? She rolled over and blinked her eyes. It was nearly pitch-black and a little cold, so she wrapped the thin blanket tighter about her body. Nathan's scent rose with the fabric, and she buried her nose to inhale even more deeply.

She was in his bedroom after he had opened up her feminine aspect or something. She didn't much care. It had felt fantastic. In fact, her body still felt as if it were vibrating—a background kind of hum that quivered at the base of her spine. All that was missing was Nathan himself.

And silence. She could hear his neighbor clearly through the wall. He was talking in a wheedling tone to someone. Wow, who'd have thought 4B could be that loud or that irritating, even through the walls?

Tracy climbed out of bed, bringing the blanket with her as she wrapped it around her naked body. It was thin and a little scratchy, but she liked the sensation. It stirred the fireflies still flitting beneath her skin. Then she saw him. Nathan was sitting in the far corner holding a flashlight on his textbook, his light blocked by his desk. He looked up as she approached.

"How are you feeling?" he asked.

She grinned. "Fantastic. You?"

"I am well, thank you." His voice was flat, his expression platonic, and Tracy felt her smile fade. The silence began to stretch only to be filled with a loud curse from the other room and the sound of a television being kicked off. She frowned.

"My neighbor," he answered, though she hadn't asked. "He likes horse racing."

"What time is it?"

"Nearly three."

"They air racing at this hour?"

Nathan shrugged. "He tapes it, studies the horses, then calls his bookie to make bets."

Tracy pursed her lips. "Guess I'm going to have to put some more soundproofing in the walls." Then she abruptly gasped. "Three in the morning! The football game. I can't believe I slept that long."

He reached to his side and picked up her cell phone, handing it over to her. "I used your cell phone. I didn't mean to pry but your brother kept calling. I think he was very worried about you."

"My brother called—"

"I texted him with your phone. I told him you were exhausted and fell asleep."

Fear tightened her chest. "You told Joey I fell asleep in your apartment?"

"I didn't identify myself except as a tenant. He was worried about you, wondered if he should come home, but I texted that you were working on plumbing repairs and fell asleep. I hope that's all right."

She nodded absently, moving through the messages between Nathan and her brother. It ended with Joey saying he'd spend the night at Tommy's again, that they'd catch up in the morning. In short, all was well. Joey didn't have to know what she'd been doing with the anonymous tenant unless she wanted to tell him. And Nathan had been unfailingly kind in both letting her sleep and covering for her with her brother.

It was the kind of sweetness she expected from a boy-friend. Except Nathan was acting nothing like a lover right then. He was wearing a thin T-shirt pulled taut over his sculpted torso and a loose gray pair of sweatpants. His bare feet seemed large and strangely sexy. In short, he was dressed the part—even giving her every iota of his attention—but there was a coldness in the air that had nothing to do with the weather.

She slowly sank onto a cushion, but she had no idea what to say. How did you ask a man if he'd suddenly lost interest? "Um…so you're studying, huh?"

He nodded and for a moment Tracy caught a flash of anguish in his eyes. He gave her no other clue as he sat as still as a statue, the only sign of life in the intensity of his dark gaze.

"Nathan, what's going on? Why won't you talk to me?"

"I… How do you feel?"

"I already told you. I feel fantastic. How do you feel?"

"Your yin energy is very strong." His expression softened. "It buzzes in my mind and gives me such joy."

Joy was good. "So why so serious?"

He sighed and his softness disappeared. "I have contacted my mother in Hong Kong. She leads the temple there." He swallowed. "She has matched you with a new teacher. He is one of the best and has guided many tigresses to the immortal realm."

A chill entered her body and she wrapped the blanket even tighter. "A new teacher. I don't understand."

"Your yin gates are open. You have wakened your tigress, and as such have passed well beyond the initial stages of training. It is now time for the next level."

"So you teach me."

He shook his head, his gaze canting away from her. "I can't."

Her jaw clenched and her shoulders tightened, but she kept her voice low despite the noise still coming from his neighbor's. "Nathan, I need a little more explanation than wham, you're dumping me."

His eyes flashed to hers. "I am not dumping you! The temple has rules that have existed for generations. The first teacher can never, ever be the second."

"Why?"

His face didn't move, but his hands did. His fingers clenched on his textbook so tightly that he ripped the page partially out of the binding. When he noticed what he had done, he slammed the book shut with a curse. Then he abruptly pushed to his feet, his gaze cold as he practically spit out his words. "It is the rule."

She watched him move to the sink of his kitchenette and angrily run water into a kettle that he banged onto a hot plate. She didn't know what to think. He was obviously upset. But about what? That he could no longer teach her? Or that she wasn't simply accepting his decree and moving on?

Tracy slowly stood, startled to realize that for all the physical intimacy they'd shared, she really didn't know him that well. "I don't want a teacher—you or anyone. I just want you. As a boyfriend."

He glanced at her in alarm. "You are a tigress. You cannot go back now. I told you that before we opened your yin gates. You have to study!"

"Or what? I'll go insane? Nymphomania? Psycho killer?"

He nodded, his expression grave. "All those are possible." He took a step forward then abruptly stopped. "I will give you Dragon Stephen Chu's e-mail address and phone number. He is very experienced and very wealthy. He will pay for your ticket to Hong Kong. You will stay at the temple for the initial orientation, and then later you will move into his home on Repulse Bay." He lifted his chin, but didn't quite meet her eyes. "It is a very exclusive neighborhood. His villa overlooks the water."

"So I'm to become some playboy's mistress." She folded her arms across her chest. "I don't think so."

He cursed long and fluently in guttural-sounding Chinese. It came from deep in his throat and sent startled shivers down her spine. "Get it out of your head that this is sex," he growled as he stalked closer. "It has nothing to do with sex or depravity. Stephen is the best teacher for you!"

"I don't want him!" She abruptly released her hold on the blanket, letting it slip away. It was an obvious ploy, but all she had as she reached up to touch his face. Her fingers trembled, but then so did his lips as she stroked across their full texture. "I want you."

She would have leaned in for a kiss then, but he refused. He held her away though his grip trembled slightly on her arms. "Why?" he pressed. "What do you intend? Do you think we will have a relationship?"

She stopped cold, realizing that yes, she had indeed thought that.

His gaze flashed fire then abruptly darkened to a cold, flat black. "To progress as a tigress, you need to cut ties with the teacher. You cannot keep your energy—your personal power—if you give it to your instructor. You cannot use it to reach the immortal realm if you give it all to me."

Tracy released a huff of true frustration. "I don't understand a word of—"

"Listen to me!" His hands tightened where he held her, and she thought he might shove her away. Either that or jerk her into his arms. But he did neither. He simply held her tightly and spoke, each word like tiny daggers. "You have the potential to become a goddess among humans! A goddess! But not if you give your power away."

She shoved him away, her eyes burning with unshed tears as she picked up the blanket. "I have no power," she muttered. "You did it all. I just—"

"Do not lie! Not to me and not to yourself!" Nathan's voice vibrated with a power she'd never heard. It locked her in place and even silenced his neighbor. Then he came around to her to wrap the blanket gently around her shoulders. "Do you truly deny the power that you felt earlier? Do you really think you have nothing?"

"I experienced some amazing things," she whispered. "But you were the one who did it. I did nothing but enjoy."

He sighed. "I did nothing but open the door to your power." Then he touched her chin, gently lifting her gaze to his. "I. Did. Nothing." He shook his head. "Compared to you, I have nothing. I will not hold you back because I am inadequate."

She stared at him, her eyes narrowing as she studied his expression. "You're lying," she whispered. "I don't know how I know it, but you're lying. You have plenty of power. There's something else."

His eyes widened in shock, but he didn't deny her words. In the end, he fell backward to lean against his desk, his shoulders slumped in defeat. She felt her belly tense in fear.

"You wish us to be lovers? I would love that more than anything, but I am a student here for another twenty months. After that, I will work in high industry for as much money as I can find. And you, where will you go to be a stockbroker? It will not be here."

"I still have to go to school! We'll figure out—"

He didn't wait for her thoughts. "And what of your college dreams? Do you intend to go to school here?"

She bit her lip. She'd been thinking of a different school. One in New York. "I don't have to be a stockbroker," she said softly.

"And then what? Will we marry? Will you leave everything you have to go with me?"

Her breath hitched in her chest. "Marry?" she squeaked. "Isn't that jumping the gun a bit?"

"So you would give yourself nightly to a man when there was no future in it?"

She straightened, twisting around to face him. "Now just a minute here! Why wouldn't there be a future—"

"Our lives are in flux right now. It is irresponsible to enter a relationship that cannot work out in the long term."

"Irresponsible?" Her voice started to rise, but she controlled it, her mind working fast for all that she'd just woken up. "Listen to me, buster, I've had boyfriends before. Irresponsible, my ass. You're turning tail and running. I want to know why."

"Dragons do not run!" he said in his most stiffly formal tone.

"Well, I've got a pretty clear picture of your backside right now," she snapped. "And it looks like you're running scared."

His eyes narrowed. He rose up from his desk, his motions smooth and infinitely powerful. He was like a god rising from the depths and she hadn't even realized she was talking to one. And worse, he was angry. Tracy took an instinctive step backward but he pursued her. His words were low—almost hissed—but she felt every syllable all the way through to her soul.

"You are a tigress. I am a dragon."

She threw up her hands, but the motion was weak and trembly. "Tigress smigress. I don't even know what that means."

He took another step forward, his words growing softer and more potent with every step. "It means you belong in the temple, tigress."

"Me in Hong Kong." She folded her arms. "Not gonna happen."

"In Hong Kong," he repeated, his voice cold and hard. "There, you will study with the best. You will become divine and will gift many others with your wisdom. It is what tigresses do," he pressed. "Whether they wish it or not, whether they understand it or not, they all end up there."

She planted her hands on her hips. "I'm not going to Hong Kong!"

He straightened, and for a moment his eyes flashed understanding, even regret. "Yes," he said softly. "You will. You will not be able to avoid it."

"Bull—"

"Then how will you balance your energies again? You have gone beyond what I can give."

She swallowed, her mind zipping back to her last week. She didn't want to repeat last week ever again. She did not want to lust after her brother's friends or hunger desperately for someone to satisfy her cravings. "You're lying," she said, but she feared what he said was true. "You're a dragon. You can satisfy a tigress."

Nathan shook his head. "I can—for a time—but you need training. And I do not have the time to spend on you right now." He glanced at his books. "I have already told you how hard it is for me to read English books. I am here for an education, not to train you."

She took a deep breath, the truth slowly slipping into her consciousness. "I was right. All along, I was right."

He frowned, obviously confused by her abrupt change of tone.

"This was a scam, wasn't it? You get a woman into your bed. You do... You do stuff to her. And then, wham, you dump her. Does it give you a feeling of power to have her beg?" Tracy swallowed back her tears. She was not, not, not going to cry.

She spun around, searching for her clothing. It was too dark. She couldn't see a damn thing through the tears she refused to let fall. But she heard. She heard him curse again in Chinese, the words low and primal. It sent a shiver up her spine and she felt another stirring in her belly. Oh, god. She couldn't be getting horny. Not now. Not again. *What the hell is wrong with me?*

She heard him sigh. The sound came from deep within him—all short and harsh and very male. He was frustrated. Well, so was she. And yet, for a moment she stopped just to hear it again. Did he really feel as bad as she did?

Then she felt him. His hands settled on her shoulders. It shocked her that while she was blindly searching through his apartment for her clothes, he could step up silently behind her and touch her. She shivered, his warmth sliding deep into her body, calming her shattered nerves. It was like that first time in the hallway when he'd taken her hands. All the chaotic emotions slowly calmed. She was still angry and close to tears, but inside, she was quieter. And because she was quiet, she could hear his words.

"You *are* a tigress. Whether you understand it or not, you are. Your place is at the temple, learning to understand and control your power."

"My horniness," she corrected.

"That is part of your power, yes, but you are so much more." He pressed a kiss at the top of her shoulder and she gasped in reaction. Lord, one touch from him and she was shivering in delight. "Why do you fight this? Don't you want to know what you can do?"

"Of course, I do," she whispered. "But what about love? Nathan, could you love me?" She knew for damn sure that she could love him.

He stepped backward, taking away his touch, removing his heat, and she shivered at the loss. "Would you choose love over immortality, Tracy? Imagine for a moment that you could become a goddess."

She spun around to face him. "Don't be ridiculous—"

"That you could heal with a touch, impart the secrets of immortality, that you could walk among the divine. Would you give that up for love?"

She folded her arms across her chest. "It's not possible."

"It is possible," he countered firmly. "And you have the talent. Can you really walk away from that? Without exploring further, could you simply turn your back on it for a love that might never be? You do not even know me well. We might hate each other in a few days' time."

Put like that, of course not. "Why do I have to choose right now? Why can't I explore both?"

Nathan sighed and gestured to his textbook. "I have a goal. It does not include a girlfriend." He looked up, an apology in his eyes. "And you have more than you can handle right now. Tigress teachings, your education, and a brother about to graduate from high school. Why would you stop moving forward now to play with a boyfriend?"

She didn't answer. She simply looked at him long and hard and forced herself to see the message behind his words. His reasons didn't matter. He didn't want a relationship with her. "So it's over before it ever begins."

He shrugged. "Why begin a path when you already know the ending will be bad? You don't understand it right now, but I have seen it dozens of time. You are a woman now with human loves and concerns. But the more your tigress awakes, the more your mind will be on immortality. Right now you think you want me. In another week, I will be a fond memory. And within a year…" He shook his head. "I will be nothing to you."

She bit her lip, trying to hold back the tears. "You must think I'm a horrible person. Why would you think I'm like that?"

He lifted his chin. "I know tigresses, Tracy. And you…" He looked at her, adoration in every line of his face and body. "You are one of the best. Even without training, you are beyond my imagination."

She turned, spotting her clothing neatly folded in a corner near his bed. "Then you have a very limited imagination."

"No," he whispered as she went to dress. "No, I don't."

# *11*

"HEY TRACY, SORRY ABOUT the delay. Been closing out a big case. But I've dug up some interesting things on your tenant. How 'bout we meet at your building at one? Cheers!"

Tracy frowned at her phone and hit the replay button on her cell. Yup, same message from Detective Michael McKay—the police officer and good friend she'd begged to investigate Nathan Gao more than a week ago.

She'd been anxious to get information on Nathan then, to find out if he had a criminal record. Well, it sounded like something was up. Unfortunately, Tracy wasn't sure she really wanted to know. She just wanted to stop thinking—dreaming—about the man.

She stared at the time. Noon. Hell. She'd slept through the entire morning. After leaving Nathan's apartment in the very early hours, she'd collapsed onto her bed and sobbed herself to sleep. And had apparently slept through Mike's call. She shoved herself upright, then made her way to the bathroom.

There was still time to catch Mike. She could come up with some lame excuse for not meeting him, but did she really want to hide from the truth? Well, yes. She didn't want to learn that Nathan was just a con man. Or maybe she did. She needed the truth. Especially now when she could still think relatively clearly. If she waited too long and got hit by that damn horny lightning again… Well, then she was doomed. She'd be at Nathan's door on her knees begging him to do anything he wanted to her. She had to know the truth now. Therefore, she had to stop moping, haul tail into the shower, and then meet Mike.

An hour later, she had her toolbox in hand and was trudging up the building staircase while guilt burned in her stomach. Mike—Detective McKay—was all business beside her, oblivious to the fact that his every word felt like another weight on her soul.

"Near as I can tell, his mother runs a high-class prostitution ring in Hong Kong. Men and women. No action too depraved so long as the money's there. The authorities have been keeping their eye on his mother, but there's never been an arrest. Though apparently she's been spending money like water lately. Just in the last few months."

Tracy did a mental calculation. "Mom" had probably started spending the moment Nathan had left home to come to the U.S. She wondered how long that well was going to last. "What is she buying?"

Mike shrugged as they reached the landing outside Nathan's apartment. "Silks, makeup, jewelry. Nothing outrageous, but it still adds up."

Mike stepped back as Tracy joined him in the hallway. He touched the small of her back, guiding her to Nathan's door. It was nothing unusual. Mike was a touchy-feely kind of guy. He didn't mean anything by it, and yet Tracy felt a zing of electricity up her spine. She and Mike had grown up together. They were friends, and frankly, she had zero interest in him as a lover. But he was a big, strong man. He had large hands and likely a big, thick cock. And…oh, my God! Tracy gasped and reordered her thoughts.

Was this what being a tigress was all about? Unbounded thoughts about young football players and big handsome cops? Fortunately, she wasn't lusting after Mike. She was just hyperaware of how his anatomy was probably constructed. Still…eww!

"Tracy? You okay?"

She blinked. "Yeah, I'm fine. So, um, that's it? All you wanted to tell me was that his mother is suspected of running a prostitution ring?" Relief colored her tone.

Mike grinned. "Well, that and to get some proof of evildoing." He gestured to Nathan's door. "So open up. And by the way, I can't tell you how grateful the department is that you noticed this guy. The last thing we need is a Chinese organized-crime outfit gaining a foothold here."

She didn't move except to fiddle with her master key. "What if the police are wrong? I mean, it could be…you know…a religion or something."

Mike laughed, his expression warm and a little bit condescending. "Yeah, I got your religion right here. Come on, Trace, let's get this show on the road."

She nodded, but couldn't force herself to open the door. "He might be home, you know."

Mike frowned. "You said he was at class."

He probably was, but she could hardly say she was feeling guilty for violating a potential felon's privacy.

"And you've got that clause explicit in the lease that lets you enter to make repairs, right?"

She nodded. Mike had even made her bring her toolbox, which hung like a lead weight in her left hand. "He said the garbage disposal doesn't work."

# Get FREE BOOKS and FREE GIFTS when you play the...

# LAS VEGAS
## GAME

*Just scratch off the gold box with a coin. Then check below to see the gifts you get!*

**YES!** I have scratched off the gold box. Please send me my **2 FREE BOOKS** and **2 FREE GIFTS** for which I qualify. I understand that I am under no obligation to purchase any books as explained on the back of this card.

351 HDL ENV4                    151 HDL EN24

FIRST NAME          LAST NAME

ADDRESS

APT.#          CITY

(H-B-01/08)

STATE/PROV.          ZIP/POSTAL CODE

| 7 | 7 | 7 | Worth TWO FREE BOOKS plus TWO BONUS Mystery Gifts! |
| | | | Worth TWO FREE BOOKS! |
| | | | TRY AGAIN! |

www.eHarlequin.com

Offer limited to one per household and not valid to current subscribers of Harlequin® Blaze®. All orders subject to approval.

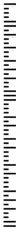

**BUSINESS REPLY MAIL**

FIRST-CLASS MAIL    PERMIT NO. 717    BUFFALO, NY

POSTAGE WILL BE PAID BY ADDRESSEE

**HARLEQUIN READER SERVICE**
**3010 WALDEN AVE**
**PO BOX 1867**
**BUFFALO NY 14240-9952**

NO POSTAGE
NECESSARY
IF MAILED
IN THE
UNITED STATES

"There you go," he answered as he pulled a wrench out of her toolbox. "And I'm an old friend just hanging out." He hefted the wrench like a weapon and grinned at her just like when they were kids. "All perfectly legal."

Just not entirely moral. Unless Nathan really was a member of an organized-crime syndicate. A very unsuccessful one. "I don't think that's possible," she hedged. "I think I was very wrong about him."

Mike smiled and gently pulled her passkey from her hand. "How 'bout we leave the question of guilt to the professionals? You just fix his sink, and I'll hang around noticing things." His gaze abruptly sharpened. "Unless there's something you're not telling me."

She shook her head. "Nothing, Mike, I just feel weird about this."

"That's why you're a landlord, not a cop." He grinned as he opened the door. "Hello? Housekeeping! Anybody home?"

She rolled her eyes. Mike sure liked catching bad guys. She followed him into the apartment, her eyes immediately absorbing the familiar surroundings. "Mr. Gao?" she called, half hoping, half dreading to see Nathan. "I'm here to fix the sink."

Silence. Well, silence except for the neighbor in 4B. This time the sound coming through the wall was a basketball game and another loud argument over the phone.

Mike frowned, obviously listening hard. "How come we can't hear that in the hallway?"

She shrugged. "Soundproofing. I must have missed the wall between the two apartments."

"I guess so." He gestured to the bookcases, cushions and perfectly made bed. "He always this neat?"

"Yeah, I think so."

Mike wandered over to the bookcase, scanning the titles with a leer. "Look at this. *Sexual Secrets of the White Tigress. Tantrism for Beginners*. Yeah, our boy here is up to his mother's tricks."

"They're just books," she snapped. "And lots of people are Tantric. Sting, for one."

"Because people always get their religious guidance from a rock star." He pulled a book off the shelf and flipped through it. "Sex books right next to accounting texts. Business school for madams."

Tracy dropped her toolbox with unnecessary force. "You don't know that. Maybe he's legit."

"Sure, he is," Mike said as he tilted a book to her. "And I'm sure Mother Teresa often preached orgasms to see God." He snorted. "Like anyone would believe this crap!"

Tracy sidestepped the tears that threatened and moved straight to righteous indignation. "You've already made up your mind about him. Just because Tantrism is different doesn't mean—"

"Is this his laptop?" Mike knelt down to where Nathan's computer rested on the floor near where he'd been studying the night before. The screen was up but dark.

"I think so," Tracy said.

Mike tapped a key and the screen powered up. It had been in sleep mode. "Well, look at that, it's still on. There is a God." He sat down on the floor right where Nathan had been last night.

Tracy turned to the sink, unable to watch. The sense that she was betraying Nathan made her physically ill. "I'll just go fix the disposal," she murmured.

Mike gave her a distracted wave. Meanwhile, the

neighbor cursed loudly and vehemently before killing his television. Apparently, his team had just lost.

They were there for another hour. The disposal was in pieces before Mike leaned back with an enigmatic expression. "I gotta get back. We'll talk more later."

Tracy put down her wrench. "Wait a minute! Did you find anything?"

Mike wouldn't answer. He just waved at her and disappeared out the door before she could press for more. She stared at her friend's retreating back, refusing to bellow after him, and in that moment, Tracy came to her own decision. If she wanted to know more about Nathan, then she would have to find out her own way. They could talk like normal people. She could ask her own questions. She could...

She wiped off her hands on a rag then grabbed her car keys. Forget Mike. She had her own idea. But first she had to get home and grab a few things.

SHE WAS IN HIS APARTMENT when he came home. Somehow Nathan knew she would be. That was why he'd gone to the library after class, then loitered in the back of a Chinese restaurant, hoping to pick up an illegal busboy job. The answer was no, but he'd tried. Then he'd finally faced the inevitable and headed home long after she would normally have left for the day.

But she was there. Not in the downstairs hallway, but in his kitchen, putting away tools while the scent of some very American-looking casserole filled the tiny apartment. She looked up as he entered, her eyes lighting with delight even though her body posture seemed reserved.

"Welcome back!" she said. "I put in a new garbage disposal. Yours was toast."

He nodded, but couldn't speak. Her beauty hit him sideways like that—catching him unaware even when he expected it. It wasn't that she was dressed to seduce. Far from it. She wore grubby jeans and a grimy T-shirt. Her face was flushed from her exertions and her hair was tied back in a ponytail that caught most but not all of her wavy tendrils. But the life flowing from her soul hit him straight in the solar plexus. She was alive and vibrant, and so damn beautiful she stole his breath.

"I made dinner. The disposal took longer than I expected. Do you mind if I use your bathroom? I just need to change clothes."

He stared at her a moment, his sense of humor finally surfacing. "No problem. But I don't remember any plans for tonight."

"High-school gym. Girls' volleyball, to be exact. Joey's there to watch his girlfriend. I thought we'd eat, watch the match, then go out for ice cream afterward."

He arched his eyebrows. "You did, did you?" How different she was now from last night when the pain from his rejection had rolled off her in waves. Today she was casual. Controlled. Suspiciously so. "Why?"

Tracy straightened to face him square-on, her shoulders stiff with tension. She wasn't as calm as she pretended. "I had a revelation while I was fixing your sink."

He blinked, his mind whirling. Was she already getting divine messages? Had she progressed that far as a tigress?

"We went too fast. I mean, I don't regret it or anything, but we don't know each other well enough yet to decide about anything. So I thought we'd just go out. We'd learn about each other's families. We'd, you know, talk as friends. We can do that at a volleyball game."

Yearning burned through his belly. "It won't work," he said to himself more than her. "You are a tigress. I cannot—"

"Yadda yadda," she interrupted. "Give me this Stephen's e-mail address. I'll contact him on your laptop if you like." She swallowed. "And there's this other thing, too. I have some questions. I...I don't want to keep noticing men. I mean, Hugh Jackman is one thing, but every healthy guy that walks by? No. So how do I stop it?"

"You train at the temple in Hong Kong," he answered wearily. Then he turned away rather than show her how much he really did ache for her. "It has been a very long day." A long day of regret. Of dreaming about what might have happened if her inner tigress had never woken. If they could have met and dated and talked as friends first. "I don't really feel—"

"Just friends, Nathan. Are you telling me you don't want a friend?" Her voice trembled slightly. "That you don't want *me* as a friend?"

"Tigresses don't have friends," he answered automatically. And once again, the message was for himself, not her. She would learn the truth about that soon enough.

"Well, then, I guess I'm not a tigress."

He looked at her. She held her head high, but the color had leeched from her face. He was hurting her, but he didn't see how he could do this—be friends and then lose her. And yet, he couldn't stand strong against her pain. The truth was he'd happily take whatever tiny piece of her he could have, but that way lay disaster. How could he be friends without wanting more? Without spending his nights wrapped in torment?

"Tracy…" he began, reaching for the only excuse he had. "Even volleyball games cost money. I don't have—"

"Oh, God, you're not going to go all annoying for five bucks? I'll pay—"

"No!" He spun around, allowing pride and frustration to cover other more vulnerable feelings. "Allow me some self-respect. I have nothing to offer you. I can't take you out on dates the way you deserve. I have no money. I can't teach you—it's forbidden. I can't even pay you my rent next month! And that…" He gestured angrily at her casserole. "That will be the first real meal I've had since coming to this country."

She paled. Her mouth worked, but no sound came out.

He rubbed his hand over his face, humiliated by his outburst. Then to make matters worse, his stomach rumbled, cutting loudly into the silent room.

Tracy laughed—a soft snort of humor that had him smiling in return. She stepped to the counter and lifted off the tinfoil covering. It was meat loaf and sauce covered by macaroni and cheese. A bizarre combination, but his mouth watered just looking at it.

"Eat while I change," she said. "We'll talk when I get out." She grabbed a sports bag near her toolbox and headed for his bathroom. He watched her go, slowly losing his mind to the beauty of her walk, of the way her hair bounced as she spun. Then she turned and looked at him, her eyes huge and her voice almost too quiet to hear.

"All I want is a little time with you as friends. That doesn't cost a dime." Then she disappeared into the bathroom.

He sighed, knowing he'd already lost the battle. He had

no business spending more time with her. She would distract him from the business of study and of finding a way—any way—to survive in the U.S.

He ought to spend the evening visiting sorority houses to offer Tantric classes. It was the very best time to pick up students. College girls without a date leaped at the chance to "expand their sexual understanding." At ten dollars a class, he could make a hundred or more with the right pitch. But not if he was watching volleyball and eating ice cream with Tracy.

Giving in to his hunger pangs, Nathan scooped up a generous portion of her meat loaf concoction. It looked very strange to his Chinese eyes, but one bite had him raising his brows in surprise. It was good. Very good. Very American, but also…

The water in his bathroom turned on. He had almost managed to forget that Tracy was a few meters away stripping naked, but the sound of the water kicked his mind into overtime. She had a water-element body, but earth ran strong through it, as well. It complimented her, making her body lush and fertile. Worse, it called to his air-element soul, begging him to breathe life where there was potential, to give space to that which was clogged. And what she gave to him! Her yin rain cooled his tendency to overheat, and her earthy strength grounded him where his own efforts left him spinning aimlessly.

In short, they matched, and if she were not the most promising novice tigress in an age, nothing could prevent him from pursuing her. But she was a tigress with a bigger destiny, though she didn't understand it. And he had his own responsibilities to his family that he had no wish to set aside.

He said that over and over; he repeated it to himself

even as he wandered to the bathroom door. His head dropped against the thin wood, listening to the changes in sound as she turned off the water. He heard her duffel bag unzip and soft thumps as she moved.

Maybe it was possible, he lied to himself. Maybe he could be just friends with a tigress and not get hurt. Maybe his heart wouldn't be torn from his chest when she abandoned him for the greater lure of heaven. Maybe…

By the time she came out of his bathroom, he had convinced himself that he could afford one night with a friend.

# *12*

NATHAN SMILED AS SWEET, cold ice cream exploded across his tongue. He rarely got to eat pistachios in Hong Kong, much less pistachio ice cream. He shouldn't be eating it now given that one scoop of the stuff cost three times a bowl of rice. But this tasted better, and he was enjoying the company—even big, burly brother Joey.

The four of them sat at a table in the Marble Slab next to the movie theaters. The volleyball game had been fun. While Joey had stood with his football teammates and grunted school cheers for his girlfriend, Nathan and Tracy had talked about inconsequential things. She had spoken with pride of her brother's achievements and told a story of her first experiences with plumbing. He had shared about trying to get any plumbing at all to the temple when the road was a tiny cart track.

And as the conversation continued, his esteem for her deepened. Not only could she talk about her own hardships with humor, but she listened—really listened—to his experiences. She laughed when appropriate, and beneath her smiles, he felt an understanding grow. She knew how hard it was to keep a large, old building functional. She squeezed his hand, saying without words that she knew how the unending list of repairs wore on a person. How bills and aches piled up. But at least he'd had his siblings, his aunt and various students to help him. She'd done it alone, without guidance or support, and for that he admired her to no end.

Now they were eating ice cream before Joey and Mandy left for the late showing of the newest blockbuster. But first, Joey apparently felt he had to give Nathan the third degree just like any good brother would for his only sister. Nathan didn't mind—much—because every question pointed out yet another reason he and Tracy wouldn't suit. And after the wonderful time he'd had at the volleyball game, Nathan needed the reminder.

"So," asked Joey, his shoulders hunching over his food, "how much money can a temple like yours pull in?"

"Very little," Nathan answered between small, delightful bites of pistachio heaven. "My temple survives at subsistence level."

Joey raised his head, his brows arching. "But you've got a good job, right? To pay for school."

"No," Nathan answered smoothly. "My fellowship fell through and I'm looking for something—anything—that will pay my bills."

Joey twisted enough to give his sister a heavy stare though he kept talking to Nathan. "So no money. What about relatives?"

"They're none of your business, Joey," Mandy interrupted. "Jeez, let your sister date whomever she wants."

"What?" Joey returned, bristling. "They were just questions. I was just asking about his family and stuff."

Nathan smiled without comment, his gaze traveling back to Tracy. She had also bristled when her brother began his not-so-subtle interrogation, but hadn't interfered. And though her shoulders stayed tight, her gaze had dropped to her food as she took tiny, tiny bites with excruciating care.

"What's it like in Hong Kong?" Mandy asked. "I'd give anything to go there. I hear the shopping's fantastic."

Nathan nodded. "If you have the money, there is no better place to buy anything."

"That's the whole problem, though, isn't it?" Joey snapped. "No money, no joy."

"That's not true!" returned Mandy with a hefty punch to his shoulder. Joey didn't even wince. "There's lots of things that don't cost a thing. The really happy people are just happy no matter what they're doing."

Nathan turned to Mandy, his esteem of the young woman rising by several notches. "That was a very enlightened statement," he said. But in his mind, he calculated the evening's tab: $13 for volleyball tickets, $20 for specialty ice cream, $14 for movie tickets. Total: $47 U.S. A fortune by his estimation, and they spent it easily as part of a regular Friday night out.

"It's all about money," Joey groused as he demolished the last of his waffle cone. "Who's got it—" He looked at his sister. "And who doesn't." He looked pointedly at Nathan.

Then Tracy spoke. She looked at her brother, her eyes warm with love, but still reflecting disappointment. "You are getting really boring, brother dear."

"And I thought you had better sense than to date—"

"Stop it!" interrupted Mandy with another punch, this one hard enough to make Joey blink. "She's right. You're being awful."

Joey subsided into a mulish silence while Mandy and Tracy applied themselves to their desserts. Nathan spoke softly, but no less clearly. "It is a brother's honored right to protect his sister. He was doing no more than I would expect from a beautiful woman's family." He sighed. "But I'm not Tracy's boyfriend. We're just friends."

All three companions stared at him in various stages of shock. Joey's expression was easiest to read. He was suspicious, but less hostile. Mandy's eyes grew misty. "That's so awesome," she said to Tracy. "He thinks you're beautiful."

"He also said he doesn't want her," Joey grumbled. "Which is total bull."

"Don't be such a hater," Mandy returned. The two began to argue in low tones. Nathan ignored them, his attention fully trained on Tracy, who had relaxed back in her seat with a calm expression.

"So now you've met my family," she drawled. "Such as it is. Tell me, does your family squabble like this? Do you take honor in protecting your sister?"

"Yes and yes," he said slowly, wondering where she intended to go with this.

"So the temple's like one big happy family? You all sit around the dinner table annoying each other? Drink out of the milk carton or chew with your mouth open or something?"

He started to nod his head, but his words came out very different. "We are a loose collection of souls—some come, some go. All have responsibilities—some gather the food, some cook it, some clean up afterward. Our meals are usually passed in silence as each contemplates her soul's state. A few have even taken vows of silence." He looked closely at her. "You will like it there. It is a beautiful place."

Joey abruptly spun around to stare hard at him. "What? What about the temple?" He turned to his sister. "You're not going to Hong Kong, are you?"

"Relax, Joey," Tracy answered smoothly. "I'm just asking about his home." She said the words, but Nathan heard the hesitation in her voice even if her brother did not. Then she tossed her plastic spoon in her empty ice-cream cup and turned back to Nathan. "What about your natural siblings? You said you have a sister and brother."

"My mother had three children, I am the eldest. Plus a few cousins who come and go."

"Very fluid, huh?" That came from Joey, the suspicion back in his voice. "No real family ties."

Nathan shrugged, not knowing how to answer. "We are what we are. I miss my brother and sister a great deal." He looked at Tracy and Joey, and thought about a life with just one sibling. It seemed so peaceful and intimate. "You are very fortunate to have a brother who loves you enough to protect you."

Tracy flashed her brother a quick smile. "He's annoying, but he's mine." She leaned forward. "But who was yours, Nathan? Who protects you?"

He stiffened. "I am the eldest. It is my job to watch out for the others."

Mandy finished off the last of her shake with a slurp, then she smiled at him. "You really take that traditional stuff seriously. That's so old-fashioned, but sweet. Kinda heroic."

He looked at her, unable to form an answer. Joey just rolled his eyes and huffed, "Girls!"

Nathan focused on Tracy only to discover she was watching him with an intensity that made him uncomfortable. Had he revealed something significant? He didn't think so. But the way she stared at him made him acutely nervous.

"So, no dad, huh?" asked Joey from the side.

Nathan shook his head. "My mother is a tigress and the leader of the temple."

"Her focus is on attaining immortality, right?" asked Tracy. "She leads the temple, takes partners, and studies for ascension. Right?"

"Yes, that is the role of a tigress."

"And her children?"

"Our role is to support the temple and its students."

She nodded. "So your role is to support your mother and her goals."

He frowned, not liking Tracy's tone. "It is an honor—"

"And a responsibility," interrupted Joey. "Yeah, we got that. But where is there room for what you want to do?"

Nathan shifted his gaze between the three of them, wondering how the conversation had turned so drastically. "This is what I want to do," he said clearly. "Business school, then a good job. Why would I do all this, come to the United States to study if not for that?"

"I don't know," Tracy answered slowly. "It's just obviously so very hard. You're broke, studying night and day, saving money any way you can to survive." She shook her head. "There has to be an easier way."

Nathan shook his head. "I left the temple because I couldn't stay any longer. And it was time to further my education."

Tracy straightened, her eyes very clear. "Why couldn't you stay?"

He swallowed. It was best he told her everything. She

needed to understand. "I was kicked out of the temple," he said bluntly.

"Really," gasped Mandy. "But why?"

"I fell in love with one of the tigresses. I pursued her with single-minded devotion. I had started out as her teacher but then fell in love." He shrugged. "But she is a tigress with no interest in such things. She said I interfered with her studies, I made it difficult for her to pursue her religion. It was an easy choice for the Tigress Mother. Nothing can interfere with the pursuit of heaven, so I was asked to leave."

"I thought you said your mother led the temple." Mandy's voice was soft with compassion.

He nodded. "She does."

Joey leaned forward hard enough to make the table creak. "Kicked out by your own mother? I don't believe it."

Nathan shrugged. It didn't matter if they believed it or not; it was true. But when he focused on Tracy, he read confusion in her eyes. She shifted nervously on her seat, then spoke, her voice coming out low but very clear. "The Hong Kong police think your mother runs a prostitution ring. They think you're trying to branch out here in Champaign."

On his left, Mandy gasped in shock, and Joey abruptly straightened. His eyes narrowed and his shoulders rose. But Nathan kept his demeanor cool, his attention completely on Tracy.

"I am impressed that you could learn that so quickly and from half a world away."

She shrugged. "Gotta love it when those connections pan out."

"Is it true?" snapped Joey, his grip on his plastic spoon had tightened into a fist.

Nathan sighed. "Prostitution is a thriving industry in Hong Kong. If it were true, I would not be worrying about money or about raising my brother and sister out of poverty. And Illinois is a long, long way to go to branch out one's business."

"It's a long, long way to go just to escape a bad love affair, too," drawled Tracy.

He didn't respond. How could he explain that he wanted—needed—to put as much distance between himself and his childhood as possible. It was only because of her—because Tracy was a promising new tigress—that he had any communication with his mother at all.

Mandy was the one, this time, to continue the questions. "So why do they think you're prostitutes?"

"They're Tantrics," Tracy answered softly. "They study sex as a path to…" She shrugged. "To more." Then she shot her brother a sharp look. "And don't go there, Joey. It's not ridiculous. It's just different."

Joey pressed his lips together, but it was clearly hard for him to stay silent. Mandy, however, dimpled prettily. "I've heard about that. It's cool—if a little weird." She turned back to Nathan. "So you and your family study sex but the cops don't understand so they think you're selling sex. Except that you're god-awful poor, and they don't get it. But you do, so you're here studying to get a good job so that you can support your mother and her temple. Cool."

Nathan struggled to follow her rapid-fire English, but then gave up because she'd apparently come to her own conclusion. She was already standing up, tugging Joey along with her.

"Come on. It's almost time for the movie." She smiled

at Tracy and Nathan together. "Thanks for the ice cream. It was cool meeting you, but we gotta go. See ya!"

Joey blinked, obviously dazed by his girlfriend, but she didn't give him time to respond. She simply tugged him hard until he had no choice but to move. Within moments, they were out the door. Even before the glass door slipped shut, Tracy burst out laughing.

"Wow, does my brother have his hands full with her!" she said.

Nathan didn't answer. He was still trying to understand what had happened.

Tracy grabbed and tossed their empty ice-cream cups out. It was apparently time to go, and so he opened the shop door and waited for her to exit.

She went through with a blithe smile, and they walked together to her truck. They were only halfway there when she turned to him with a fierce expression. "I admire what you're trying to do. I really do. I understand the need to protect and support your family, but you're going to have to get over it. You know that, don't you?"

"What?"

"They've got to learn how to take care of themselves. The temple needs to be self-sufficient. Your brother and sister have to find their own way. If you pour everything you have into supporting them, then you'll have nothing left for you. You'll end up resenting them and frankly, you're not doing them any favors. It's good for kids to struggle a bit."

He stared at her a moment, stunned by her audacity. No Chinese person would ever dare say such a thing to him. But then, Tracy wasn't Chinese. "You know nothing of my family or my life in Hong Kong," he said stiffly.

She shrugged. "Maybe not. But I know kids have to be pushed out of the nest eventually. Even you."

"I *am* my family's nest!" he snapped, startled by his sudden fierce anger. "Without me—"

"They're without you right now, Nathan. How are they doing?"

He swallowed. Awful, truth be told. He had received another couple of e-mails, one from each of his siblings. Their mother was shopping again with money they didn't have.

"Nathan? How are they doing without you?" Tracy pressed.

He sighed. "Go to the temple and find out for yourself."

"Ha!" she crowed. "They're doing fine, aren't they? They're working or going to school and so your big martyr routine is nothing of the sort." She planted her hands on her hips, her eyes piercing even in the darkness. "So why all the way to the United States? Did you really get kicked out of the temple? Did you really fall in love?"

"Yes and yes." He could see that she didn't believe him. She had grown up with a loving family. She didn't understand the emptiness of having people around, but no love. "Why do you push at me, Tracy? You have everything— a brother who adores you, a future as a great tigress. Ask me about life in the temple, ask me about what happens between partners. Those questions I can answer. They are your path, and you should want to know more about it."

She started walking around more cars, cutting through a lane to get to the right aisle. He followed as fast as he could, but she was angry and moving very fast. "I'll ask what questions I want, thank you very much." She stopped abruptly beside a huge SUV and spun back to him. "What's it going to take to convince you that I'm not a tigress? That I'm not going to your temple, that I won't leap down whatever mystic path you think is so inevitable for me?" She straightened to her full height. "I choose my own path, Nathan. We all do. And I do *not* choose to be a tigress."

He looked at her, hope surging within him despite what logic and reason proclaimed. Was it possible? Could she choose to be an amazing woman, not an amazing goddess? He wanted to believe, but his experience told him differently. "A few minutes ago, did you notice the man in the running pants as he wiped sweat from his brow? Did you see his chest muscles beneath his muscle T-shirt? And what about his legs? Were you watching the way his pants hugged tight to his bottom?"

Her jaw clenched but she ground out the words. "I saw, I noticed, but I don't have to act on it."

Nathan sighed. "Not today. But you will. Without training, you will act. You belong at the temple, Tracy. It's where tigresses go."

She glared at him; she tried to stare him down, but it didn't work. Everything in him said she was a tigress and not someone who would ever form a lasting attachment with a man. Never. And so in the end, she curled her hands into fists and shook them impotently at her sides. "You are such a stubborn, arrogant prick! You think you know everything, and you don't. You just don't!" And with that she spun around and stomped away.

He was busy watching her shove her fists into her pockets, and she was busy controlling her fury. Neither of them noticed the pothole in the pavement until she had stepped in it, rolling her ankle out from under herself. He saw her hips shift as she lost her balance. With her hands deep in her pockets she couldn't catch herself, so she fell hard against the corner of her own truck. He saw it happen, was already diving forward to catch her, but he was too late.

The side of her head caught the corner edge of her truck, knocking her in a different direction as she tumbled to the ground. While he was still a step away, she hit the pavement. Her elbow connected first, then she rolled onto her back, then her other side. He saw blood and hair whip past, but mostly he saw her face contorting in surprise and pain. Her teeth were bared and her jaw clenched. She didn't even cry out.

And then he caught her. Her roll was nearly at an end anyway, but he still tried to cushion her body against his. "Tracy!"

She growled, deep in her throat. Oddly enough, the sound reassured him. She was still conscious.

"Take it easy," he said. "You hit your head." Nathan kept one hand braced on her shoulder while the other gently probed into the hair above her forehead. He felt the slick welling of blood as she flinched away.

"Ow! Stop that!" She shoved him away. "I know what happened." She rolled smoothly into a seated position, then gingerly burrowed her fingers into her hair. The blood was already dripping down her cheek. "Perfect," she groused. "Just perfect."

"We should get you to a hospital."

"Do you know what the E.R. costs?" She flinched as she looked at the blood on her hand. "It's not that deep. Head wounds always bleed a lot." She grimaced then wiped the blood off on her shirt before returning to probe her wound. "It's shallow and long."

"A hospital could stitch it up," he said gently.

"Why? To prevent a scar underneath my hair? It hurts but it's just a cut." The blood still ran in long streaks down her cheek. It looked awful, but she was right. What he had felt told him the cut was not serious.

"Very well," he acquiesced. "Give me the keys. I will take you home."

He helped her stand, feeling the strength in her body despite the blood. As they made it to their feet, she pulled out her keys but wouldn't give them to him. "What side of the road do they drive on in Hong Kong?" she asked.

He grimaced. "The left."

"Then I'm driving." She shook her head when he began to protest. "I can handle a scar under my hairline. A busted truck is something entirely different."

"But—" he began.

"Get in the car, Nathan. I'm taking you home."

He pressed his lips together feeling acutely useless. This entire evening had been a huge blow to his masculinity. He hadn't been able to pay for anything; he hadn't caught her when she'd fallen, he couldn't even drive her home. "At least drive to your home. I can walk from there."

She wadded up the end of her shirt, pulling it high to wipe the blood off her forehead. It smeared across her face in an ugly mess, but no new blood dripped down. They both waited, keeping the dome light on as they watched. After a couple minutes, she gently touched her hairline. "See," she said, "it's already stopped."

He pulled her hand away and gently blew her hair aside. "Yeah, it looks like it's slowing down."

With a nod of satisfaction, she started the engine. As she drove, he watched closely for signs of distress and found nothing. Not even his sister would handle a blow to the head with nonchalance, but Tracy didn't seem fazed.

"Quit staring. I'm fine," she said.

"I know," he answered. "I'm just…"

"Surprised? Don't be. A lack of health insurance makes one a lot more casual about injuries."

"But—"

"Leave it, Nathan. I'm fine."

He nodded, still thrown by his uselessness and her competence. She truly was an amazing woman.

She pulled into the parking lot of his apartment building and killed the engine. "Look, I know I'm in for a rough patch, trying to control my inner tigress or whatever. But I'm willing to work at it. I'll meditate, I'll read whatever stuff you want me to, but you need to understand that I am in control of my destiny. I already have a plan for my life and it doesn't include a temple in Hong Kong."

He nodded slowly, stunned to admit that it was possible. If anyone could deny the call of the tigress, it would be Tracy. She had that much strength of will. With the right training, it was possible. She could choose her path rather than let her inner passions drive her destiny.

"Okay," he finally said. "You win. I will give you what guidance I can."

She smiled brightly at him. "I knew you'd come around eventually."

"I have another book upstairs for you. Do you want to wait while I get it?"

She frowned and wiped at her forehead again. "Actually,

if you don't mind, I think I'll come up with you and use your bathroom. I feel like a disgusting mess."

"No," he answered honestly. "You are beautiful." Then he got out of the truck and rushed around the side to help her out of the cab. Too late. She was already out and wondering what was taking him so long. He smiled. "More than beautiful," he murmured. "Much, much more."

# *13*

TRACY LOOKED IN NATHAN'S bathroom mirror and gasped. She'd known there was a lot of blood, but she hadn't expected to look like a horror-flick victim. Her knees weakened, and she was grateful for the support of the bathroom counter. More important, she was thankful for Nathan's steady presence on the other side of the door. Even her big strong brother tended to freak at the sight of blood, but Nathan had been a calm, reassuring presence that helped her move from bravado into strength.

She leaned forward and tried to part her hair. It was a gory mess. Careful probing told her that she had a nice-sized lump, but the cut had already closed. Unfortunately, the blood had matted her hair. She knew from experience that the sooner she washed it out, the better all around.

She grimaced as she thought of her options. Despite her bravado, she wasn't really ready to go home to an empty house. She wanted to stay with Nathan. Maybe she could get him to open up more about his family. There was so much she wanted to learn about the man completely outside of tigress training. She'd brought up her duffel bag, so she had a change of clothes. Making a swift decision, Tracy opened the bathroom door and called to Nathan.

"Do you mind if I just shower here? I don't think anything short of that is going to help."

He was at his bookcase, flipping through a stack of books, presumably for her to read. He looked up and smiled, making her stomach do a little flip-flop. "Whatever you need."

He meant it in more ways than one, and she felt a shiver of warmth course down her spine. If they could just get past this tigress stuff, there was so much potential between them. She smiled in return and then ducked back into the bathroom, quickly stripping out of her clothing. A quick shower, some tea and then they could talk.

The water felt hot on her skin, but so welcome. She went slowly, using very little of his generic shampoo and being careful with her wound. But before long, that was done and she gave herself up to the relaxation of hot water sluicing down her body.

She heard a noise. Glancing through the semitranslucent curtain, she saw the bathroom door crack open. It was Nathan. She could see his outline clearly, but she didn't turn to look directly at him. Now that she thought about it, he might have been calling her for a while, asking if she was okay, but she'd been so involved in the simple joy of hot water that it hadn't registered.

She stole another glance at him. His expression looked tortured. Now there was a man struggling with his inner nature. She'd been up close and personal with her brother's adolescence, and she knew the look of a man in lust. He wanted her. That had never been more apparent. Even through the curtain, she could see that his fingers where white where they gripped the door. But he constantly held himself apart, throwing his tigress stuff at her as a way to keep himself distant. She knew it, and it frustrated her. The question was: how could she get him to move beyond it?

Her answer was a cheap trick, but she couldn't resist. He wanted to watch her? Fine. She would give him a show. She began by raising up her arms to rinse out her hair. Her breasts lifted up to the ceiling, and she knew he could see them tightening in desire. Then she watched out of the corner of her eye for his reaction.

He started to back away, but stopped. As if he couldn't help himself, he let go of the door and allowed it to swing slowly back open. Then he just stood there and watched—clearly mesmerized.

Tracy smiled. She had him now. Grabbing the soap, she extended one leg to the lip of the tub. It was easy to soap between her toes then slowly draw the bubbles up her ankle and over her calf. What wasn't so easy was to concentrate on a seduction without getting worked up herself. She'd never done anything like this before, even in fantasy.

But the idea that Nathan was watching her—was unable to *stop* himself from watching her—gave her new boldness. And that made her feel all the more sexy as she slicked her way up over her knee to her thigh. Her breath shortened, and her thighs trembled. But most of all, her brain froze with shock at what she saw Nathan doing. It was enough to have her drop the soap with a loud clatter.

His gaze was fixed on her, but his hand wasn't idle. She couldn't even tell if he was aware that he'd popped open the clasp to his pants and reached inside. He was stroking himself! Right there as he watched her.

She licked her lips, incredibly turned on. Her chest

started tingling and she found to her own amazement that her hand had slipped between her legs. Oh, wow did it feel good. She touched herself, but kept her eyes on him. He had pulled himself out and was fully exposed. She was even able to time her motions with his.

She was nearing the edge. She was close to coming, but she didn't want to do it alone. She wanted him, and more important, she needed him to acknowledge that he wanted her—as a girlfriend, a lover, whatever. She craved that acknowledgment. So she abruptly turned and shoved the curtain sideways, facing him dead-on. The water hit her shoulder, and she slammed it off with an impatient gesture. But her gaze remained on him where he stood frozen, his pants by his ankles, his penis in his hand.

"You want me," she said, her voice deep and throaty.

"Yes."

"And God knows, I want you right now." She stepped out of the tub, her breasts bobbing and dripping. His eyes fastened there as she touched his forearm. Water slid from her arm to his wrist, his hand, his cock. "Let me," she whispered as she licked her lips. Without waiting for his answer, she slipped her hand to his wrist then burrowed into his palm. She accidentally scraped her nail against his smooth tip and he sucked in his breath in shock. She did it again, and his fingers spasmed open.

It was better than she imagined. Thick, pulsing and hot enough to burn her hand. He groaned as she fondled it, stroking from tip to base. She was so engrossed in gripping him, in pushing back the layer of foreskin to the hungry mouth, that she was surprised to feel his hand slip between her legs.

She trembled in reaction, her gasp cutting off as he slid

between her folds. But for once, she wasn't going to be distracted. The whole problem was that he was willing to give but not receive. That was one way he kept his distance from her. So she shouldered his arm aside and dropped to her knees before him.

Finally, she got to taste! It was different than she'd expected. Salty, hot and large—yes. Those things she had read about. But he was also throbbing with energy. Like what he had done to her breasts in her kitchen, his cock felt larger than its physical space. When she licked it, she tasted his skin, but she also felt the pulse of energy flowing from him into her tongue.

It was bizarre, but it felt fabulous. He tasted like life, and she wanted more of it. She did everything she had read about and more. She licked; she nipped; she engulfed and sucked and swallowed. He put up a weak protest at first. His hands were on her shoulders, and he murmured, "We can't."

She didn't bother responding because obviously they could. She could. And when his hands shifted from a gentle push away to a hard grip, she knew he was getting close. The power that she stroked was closer, too. It was swelling in her mouth and mind. She could feel it tingling all the way through her spine, and she loved it.

"Tracy…" he gasped. "Tracy!"

She liked the sound of her name cried like that. She had one hand cupping his balls, the other slid around to his tight tush. She felt everything in him clench. It was time, and she was more than eager. With a deep pull, she felt him release. His body pumped; his semen erupted, but that was nothing compared to what she felt in her mind. It was as if her head had been engulfed in an explosion of power. It was thick; it was potent and it was all Nathan.

She felt his strength in the pure white light of it, his passion in the heat that burned through her. But underneath the explosion, she felt his quiet loyalty to those he cherished, and the sweet essence that was all him. She absorbed it all, savoring every sweet, salty taste.

And when it began to fade, she felt him drop to his knees before her. "Tracy," he whispered. "I can't refuse you anything. God, why can't I say no to you?"

She didn't know, and she didn't care. Instead, she kissed him, putting all her joy into that connection. Did he feel it? Did he know what he had given her? There wasn't time to ask as she felt him slide his hand between her thighs. She was wet and willing there, but mostly she was too dazed from his energy to fight.

"Use it," he whispered to her. "Combine my yang with your yin. Feel how potent it can be."

She didn't understand his words. She never did when he said stuff like that, but why ruin the moment with questions? Her hands were on his chest, but now she slid them higher onto his shoulders. She needed to be steadied as his fingers began their work. He slipped inside her with one finger while his thumb slid upward. His movements were quick—abrupt even—and she gasped, her bottom tightening in startled reaction. She bucked away from him, but he didn't let her escape.

He pursued her, pushing a second finger deeper inside that he wiggled in a pattern she didn't understand. But wow, did she feel it, especially as he began a long circle with his thumb. Her legs trembled. It was a good thing she was already on her knees or she would have fallen.

Then he twisted his head, taking her mouth with a fierce, possessive kiss. He thrust his tongue inside her while his fingers stroked in their own rhythm. In and out they slid, coiling and swirling against her internal walls in a way that only he understood. Her body bucked, thrusting against him harder and harder. She provided the force; he held the pattern—in her mouth, deep inside her belly, and then finally with his thumb against her clit.

Her climax roared through her. It began deep like the pierce of a burning arrow, but then it flew upward, flame searing up her spine and through her mind. With a single breath, she was wholly engulfed. And then it kept going. Up, up, up, her climax continued to expand, taking her mind and soul with it. She knew nothing but its heat and the joy that it brought.

She began to hover, still expanding, but not quite so rapidly. And in that moment of suspended breath, she felt Everything. Everything was warm like a velvet womb. Everything was alive with the pulsing beat of a heart—two hearts? A thousand million hearts? All totally suffused in love. Everything smelled like rich fertile earth and tasted like spring air after a rain shower. Everything was completely and totally wonderful!

Tracy breathed deeply, wanting to draw all of Everything inside herself. It took only a moment before she realized that she already was Everything. And what she was—what Everything was—was love. Pure, beautiful, pulsing with clarity, absolute love. She was accepted; she was perfect. Better yet, she was accepting of everything else—imperfect or perfect or perfectly imperfect. The logic of it didn't matter. The internal voice of her mind, the part of her that constantly quantified and defined and explained faded away. And in the silence, Tracy knew total love.

NATHAN HELD HER AS SHE screamed in her climax. Her body arched, everything fully contracted before shuddering in wave after wave of ecstasy. He kept it going as long as he could, intensifying the rhythm though she tried to pull away from him. He wanted her to feel, to fly, as long as possible. He wanted to give her that gift.

And then her cry stopped on a gasp. She was arched in full extension, her belly rippling and contracting about his fingers. But her breath abruptly stilled to short breathless pants.

He stared at her, seeing her frozen state and yet feeling her still gripping his fingers in the steady pump of orgasm. It wasn't possible. She couldn't be in a tigress trance, could she? And yet, the sight was unmistakable.

Tracy was ascending to heaven right this moment, and he felt a burst of fierce pride at her accomplishment. But that was quickly followed by a moment of sheer panic. She was in a trance while kneeling on a bathroom floor. A tigress in full ascent was not aware of anything beyond the blessings of the divine. She had no control of her body, was not even aware that it existed. He would have to hold her gently throughout her trance. But they were on cold tiles. Water was everywhere. And he—idiot that he was—had his pants still down by his ankles.

She needed to be lying down. She was to be kept warm and protected because a trance could last hours. But how? The scrolls said it was dangerous to disturb a tigress in such a state. He might be able to support Tracy's body for a few hours, but he couldn't guarantee it. And what if she took a chill? He had to get her to a bed and wrap her in dry towels.

As gently as possible, he withdrew from where her yin pump continued to pulse. It was as strong as when she'd first convulsed, and he repressed a groan of regret. How he wished he could be with her at this moment, his dragon deep inside her. They could fly together to the immortal realm. But that of course was not his path.

First thing he did was kick out of his pants. It was awkward and difficult with his other hand still supporting her body, but he managed it. Then he shifted her gently into his arms. She went easily, her body becoming lax except for the continuing contraction of womb and belly. He could feel the steady ripple where her abdomen pressed against him.

He lifted her slowly, doing his best not to break her meditative trance. It was difficult and took a lot of steady strength, but thankfully he had lifted many heavy things in his lifetime: firewood, buckets of water, even sick women—but none as precious as a tigress in full trance.

He walked without jarring her, his steps small glides to his bed where he set her down carefully. He dared not dry her body for fear of disrupting the trance, so he wrapped her in his sheets. He peered at her face, alert for signs of distress. None. Her eyes beneath her lids were in the steady left and right motion of deepest trance.

Without turning away, he grabbed a pair of shorts and pulled them on. He was cold. His shirt was wet where it plastered against his skin, but he didn't want to abandon her even for that short moment to change. So he knelt down on the floor beside her, watching and waiting in silent awe.

It took twenty minutes before he noticed that his knees were numb. His back began to ache soon afterward. Then awe slipped away into other thoughts. That was when it hit him. That was when Nathan realized what he had done.

He'd convinced himself that she could resist the call of a tigress. He'd told himself that they could be friends, sharing their time together outside of her sexual needs. But all he had done was let down his guard. Tracy had no understanding of how a tigress called unconsciously to a man. It was in her energy, and it slipped into a man's soul and led him along until it could pounce.

Her shower had gone on too long. He had begun to worry and had pushed open the bathroom door to see if she was okay. That was all it took. One look at her sleek, wet body and he was lost. Perhaps he could have resisted. He had told himself to step away, to back into his living room though the vision of her beneath the shower had already branded itself in his mind. He'd even learned from years in a tigress temple that sometimes a man simply had to stimulate himself or lose his mind when surrounded by so many gorgeous women. He could do that alone and never risk a deeper connection with Tracy.

But then she had begun to soap herself. Her one leg extended as her hands slipped up and over her calf, her knee, until… He could not resist that sight. He had to watch. He didn't even remember opening his pants. All he knew was a desperate hunger for her.

Then the tigress had pounced. She had slammed open the curtain and taken what she needed from him. He could not resist Tracy. And so she had taken his seed and his yang power. And he had stroked her until she'd soared to heaven—heaven!

She would abandon him now. Once a tigress danced with the divine, the men became nothing more than a source of power for their next journey. Yang seed as jet fuel. The man was a means to an end.

That was why he'd left the temple never to return. He was done with being used. But then he had met Tracy and given in again. He didn't regret her ascent, only the result. There was no hope for them now. She would abandon him. What woman—what person—would ever choose the mundane over the divine? No one. And of all people, Tracy deserved to walk among angels.

He leaned forward, touching her belly with the lightest of strokes. She was still contracting, still deep in her trance.

But it had happened so fast! And she was untrained! He'd never heard of such a thing before, never heard of anyone ascending until after years of study. He couldn't understand how this had happened. Unless… He shook his head, his eyes going to her core. Could it be? Could Tracy be a virgin? It was the only possible explanation for abilities so early in her training.

The reasons didn't truly matter. It had happened. She was a full tigress now. He sat back on his heels, watching over her tigress play. But in the darkness, he remembered his many rejections by other tigresses. Bit by bit, his heart hardened. It was time, he decided, to be done with all tigresses.

TRACY BLINKED HER EYES and wondered where she was. It was heavy here. And cold. She closed her eyes again. No, wait, they'd never really been open. She missed where she'd been. It was… It had been… Where was it?

She forced her eyes open, needing to orient herself. She saw Nathan. His gaze was trained on her, and for a moment he was suffused with such light that she blinked.

Then it was gone. He was simply a man again. A beautiful man of smooth skin and serious dark eyes. He wore
a wrinkled shirt that looked as if it had gotten soaked then
dried on his body. She couldn't see farther down because
he was kneeling beside her—beside the bed—his gaze incredibly intent on her face.

"Don't try to move yet," he said. His voice grounded
her. "You have been in the divine realm. Try to hold on
to what details you can. They will fade quickly."

"You looked… You were light and love and kindness."
She smiled. "Mom always said to find a kind man." She
blinked only to discover that her eyes were already closed.
So she opened them again. "Now you just look sad."

"Tell me what you remember."

She felt his hand, large and strong, surrounding hers
on the sheet. She wanted to twist her wrist to touch him
back, but couldn't force herself to do it. So she sighed
happily and allowed his heat to sink into her.

"Tracy? Are you in pain? Are you hurt?"

She frowned, trying to put meaning to his words. "Pain"
had no reference in her mind. Other things reigned in her
thoughts. "Lights," she murmured as her eyes drifted shut.
"Lights in harmony. They tasted like music." She tried to
float back to that special place. "I was love, Nathan. Pure,
divine love." How she ached to go back there.

"Were the lights swinging?" he asked. His voice was
low, the texture to it velvety rough. Not that velvet was
rough, but compared to what she'd been listening to, his
voice was different—like granite compared to glass. And
yet, she found she liked his voice, liked the weight of his
hand on hers, liked everything about his presence right
beside her.

With Herculean effort, she turned her hand over so she could touch him palm to palm. "Talk to me some more," she said. "Tell me about where I've been. Tell me how to go back."

She felt his other hand on her cheek, stroking gently. She gasped at his touch, but then released the breath on a sigh. Another point of warmth. Another place on her body that remembered who and where she was. She let the weight of her head press her cheek into his caress.

"I don't know where you've been," he said. "I've never gone."

"You were there." She opened her eyes. It was easy now. "I saw you and wanted to be with you."

He smiled, the expression so tender it nearly broke her heart. "And so you came back here. Where I am."

"No…" she said. "Maybe." Her eyes drifted shut again. "I don't know."

"I wasn't there, but you were. What did you see?"

"It was so fast. Thirty seconds, maybe a minute."

"You were there for nearly two hours."

She opened her eyes again and focused on the ceiling. It was shadowed and dark, and she saw nothing. "A minute, maybe a little more."

"Time in the divine realm flows differently. Or not at all. The texts are unclear."

"It was so perfect." Then she looked around. Her awareness of this place was returning. She was naked in his bed and wrapped in wet sheets. "I was in the shower. I was trying to seduce you."

"It worked," he said. "I couldn't keep my hands off of you."

She smiled. "It did work."

"Then you ascended to the antechamber. Not quite heaven but close. We call it the Chamber of a Thousand Swinging Lanterns."

Tracy lifted her head. "I remember the lights. The sound was love. How can sound be love?" It didn't make sense, but she knew it was true. There was love. Here was cold and noise and loneliness. "I want to go back."

"It is the gateway. No novice has ever been so blessed. *Never before,*" he emphasized. "I've been trying to think of why it happened—" He cut off his words, obviously stopping himself before saying something. Then she felt a swift chaste kiss on her lips. She would have deepened it, but Nathan gave her no chance. "You should rest more before moving around. Ascension takes a great deal out of a body. I will get you some of your excellent meat loaf if you think you can eat."

Meat? She grimaced. Too heavy.

"Tea, then," he said. "It will settle your energies without weighing too much."

So he left her side to wait upon her. She watched him go, trying to remember what it was she was doing, what she wanted, and why she was here. Not here in his apartment, but here in the world. She had no answers and wasn't even sure of the questions. In truth, she felt like formless potential without direction or purpose. Until he returned with her tea.

He helped her sit up, and once he touched her, all became easier. With his assistance, she unwrapped the wet sheet, opening up to the air as she settled against the headboard. Her breasts bobbed as she moved, and the room felt very cool on her bare skin, but those thoughts scattered when he pressed a steaming mug into her hands.

Tracy inhaled deeply, trying to draw the steam into her body. But what she felt most were Nathan's hands around hers, his breath as it touched her forehead, and the sight of his large toes. She was looking down at the mug when she saw his lower half. First the long basketball shorts in Illini-orange, lean shins with well-formed calves, and then his solid feet and manly toes. Yes, manly toes. The toes were broad; the nails were blunt, and there was absolutely no hair anywhere that she could see.

She blinked, startled at what she was noticing, what she had never seen until now. She lifted her gaze to his. "Can I go back there again?"

He stiffened. She might not have noticed but she was watching him closely. "Drink."

She did, but she never broke eye contact. In the next apartment, Nathan's neighbor switched on his television. Tracy winced and her mind kicked into gear. She began thinking about the cost and time it would take to soundproof the wall. "It's noisy here," she murmured. "It was so quiet there." She huffed in disgust. "The details are fading."

He sat back on his heels, watching her with guarded eyes. She sipped her tea and struggled with her memory.

"Tracy, are you a virgin?"

She gaped at him, unable to understand his words. "What?"

"Have you ever had a man penetrate you? It's the only explanation why it happened so fast, so early in your training. A virgin's energies are stronger, more pure."

Any residual heavenly glow faded. She became well and truly grounded here. Instead of answering, she shifted her legs off the bed. "I'm going to get dressed now."

"You need to rest. Many tigresses remain in bed for days after ascending."

She didn't even dignify that with an answer. Instead, she pushed to her feet, pleased when she made it with only a tiny case of the dizzies.

He held her by the elbow to steady her, and she didn't throw him off. She was too busy smelling the sweet warm scent of him. God, she liked his smell.

"Please, Tracy, answer the question. It's important."

She opened her eyes and grimaced at him. "My hymen is *not* intact. Happy?"

He shook his head. "A man, Tracy. Has a man ever penetrated you?"

She stared at him. It was ridiculous to feel embarrassed about this, but she was. Unfortunately, there was no compromise in his tone or expression. "I've been Joey's mom since I was eighteen. It's not so odd."

His free hand touched her face, and she was startled to realize that he trembled. "You are the rarest of the rare. Your tigress is awake, Tracy, and you are still untouched by a man. No wonder you can travel to the immortal realm."

"You've touched me." She jerked her arm out of his grip.

"Yes, and I probably should not have. I probably weakened—"

It was abruptly too much for her. This place was too confusing, too hard, and she hated it. "Stop it! Just stop it!" she screeched. "I don't get you, Nathan. You push me away, you bring me close. You touch me and I go amazing places, and then you say we shouldn't have." She pressed her hands to her head. "I don't understand any of this!"

"Calm down," he said, his voice low enough to be soothing. "The texts say that a return from heaven is unsettling to even the most experienced tigress. She wants to return to heaven, and yet she is stuck on Earth. It tends to create anger and fury."

She dropped her hands and glared at him. "I am angry at you. It has nothing to do with…with…that other place." Except maybe he was right. Everything there had made sense. Everything was love. Here was confusion and separation. "I am so alone," she whispered.

He closed the distance between them in a heartbeat. His arms came around her, and she was once again enfolded in his warmth. She hated herself for closing her eyes, for leaning into his strength, but she needed it deep in her core.

"You should rest," he murmured against her hair. She stiffened and shook her head.

"I don't need to sleep." She needed the world to make sense. She needed *him* to make sense, but that was too far a stretch. "I think I should go home." At least there she could think. Maybe even remember.

Nathan sighed. "I will drive you. I will even remember to drive on the right side of the road."

She nodded. She wasn't in any condition to drive herself. With his help, she managed to dress with some semblance of her dignity. He was unfailingly kind, reverent even, and though his tender care of her was certainly nice, she wondered what had happened to her ardent lover.

"I don't like it when you treat me with awe," she said as they made it to her truck. "I'm just a person."

He didn't respond. Apparently he needed all his concentration to stay on the right side of the road. By the time he'd escorted her inside her house and up the stairs, she'd given up all hope for an answer. But then he stopped just inside her bedroom door.

"I tried, Tracy," he said. "I truly wanted to believe."

"Nathan—" she began, but he cut her off.

"We cannot see each other again. You are a tigress."

"I'm not—"

"You went to the immortal realm. You want to go back. Soon you will give everything you have, everything you are to return there." He shrugged. "I cannot compete with that."

"Of course you can," she answered. She took a step toward him, but he shied backward. "I don't want to be a tigress. I want you." She said the words, even believed them. But in her heart, she wondered if she was lying. Heaven had been…heavenly.

Nathan must have seen the doubt in her eyes because he shook his head, his eyes going flat. "You do not understand," he said, his words sounding very final. "I do not want you."

"That is such a lie," she whispered. Except, looking into his eyes, she saw only honesty.

"I lust for you, Tracy, but that is different. I can't live like this. I won't." He backed farther down the hallway. "I won't see you again." Then he was gone.

# 14

SUNDAY MORNING DAWNED beautiful, but Tracy didn't see much of it. Only enough to bury her head beneath her covers with a very large groan.

The last day and a half hadn't gone well. She'd spent most of Saturday reliving every moment she'd spent with Nathan, from those first flirty conversations through to his last words to her. "I do not want you…I won't see you again." Hard to argue with that.

Her evening had been spent sobbing over a romantic movie that hadn't made her feel one iota better. Worse, her dreams that night had been sexual replays that had turned her into a knot of frustration. By morning, she knew she couldn't face the world, so she buried her head and tried—again—to make it all go away. The doorbell chime made that plan a little harder, but she tried nonetheless. Who visited at…she peered at the clock…10:21 a.m. on a Sunday?

Nathan, that was who, knocking with regular and very insistent thunks on her door. At least that was who she hoped it was. She clambered out of bed to peek out her window. Yes, it was him. The sunlight seemed to soak into his black hair, giving him a special dark gleam. She couldn't suppress a tiny thrill of delight at the sight.

She went to grab her robe, but then changed her mind at the last moment. Let him see her in her jammies. He deserved to see her in a thin spaghetti-strap top and her flannel Men are Pigs pants.

By the time she made it downstairs, the knocking had stopped. Was he leaving? Then she heard the ring of her cell phone. He was calling her. She grinned, feeling as if for once she might have the upper hand with the man. She waited a couple moments more, then pulled open the door.

"Good morning, Nathan. Something I can help you with?" Wow, he looked good rumpled. His hair was wind tossed, falling across his forehead at a rakish angle. His jeans looked faded and threatened to slip down at the slightest provocation. But the very best part right then was the way he opened his mouth to speak but nothing came out. Not a word.

Instead, his eyes widened at her clothing, and his gaze dropped down to the outline of her tightened breasts. Yes, the outside air was cold, and Tracy really liked the sight of one gorgeous man struck dumb by the result. But not enough to forgive him for being an ass.

She smiled. "You look like you slept in those clothes."

He shook his head. "Didn't sleep. Thinking."

"Must have been some thoughts."

His gaze traveled back to her face as he appeared to shake himself out of his daze. "Um, yes. May I come in?"

"Of course." she stepped back, but not very far. Just enough to force him to pass within a hair's breadth of her as he entered.

She saw his jaw clench at her ploy. It was an obvious one, but still effective. Like a man facing a tribunal, he squared his shoulders and marched right in. Except when he would have passed her, she leaned in, brushing her breasts across the full bulk of his bicep.

It was meant to be a tease, a playful game of revenge, but long before the fireflies did more than an initial flutter, Nathan spun around. He slammed the door shut with one hand while his body pinned her against the wall. She gasped in surprise, but all too soon other sensations pounded into her blood.

There was no fat on his body. She felt the tense grip of his chest and the powerful trap of his arms as he braced himself on either side of her head. Below, his jeans were amazingly soft, allowing her to feel the hard ram of his erection against her groin. His thighs were spread wide enough for his legs to pin her, and when she tried to shift, she found no give at all. He could have been made of stone.

"Nathan…" she gasped. The scent of him was beginning to make her dizzy.

"Don't play with me today, tigress. I have been awake all night thinking of you—"

"That makes two of us," she murmured, unable to stop herself from lifting her face to his, from teasing her lips across his. "For a man who doesn't want me, you seem to be standing awfully close."

"I never said I didn't want you," he growled. Yes, a real honest to goodness growl that settled in her belly and quivered there.

"So take me," she answered as she nipped at his bottom lip.

He needed no more invitation. He possessed her mouth like a warrior staking his claim. He thrust into her; he opened her wide, and he then he plundered her mouth as never before. He was normally so self-contained, she was unprepared for the primal power in his kiss.

Tracy raised her arms. She couldn't reach his face—his arms blocked the way—but she could burrow beneath his shirt and feel every lean, rippling inch of his chest. "Oh, God," she gasped when they broke for air. "Nathan, I… Oh!"

He shoved her top down to her waist in one powerful jerk. Then he once again planted his hands on either side of her shoulders. She remained trapped, though he did widen his arms as he slid lower on her body. His mouth claimed her nipple. He suckled; he toyed; he nipped until she arched beneath him.

"Nathan…" she breathed.

"Where's your brother?" he rasped against her skin.

"What?"

"Joey!" he demanded as he took her other nipple in his mouth.

"Gone. School lock-in."

His answer was a satisfied grunt. Then he dropped his arms to rip her pants down to her ankles. A second later he gripped her hips and hoisted her high, leaving her pajama bottoms on the floor.

She didn't have the presence to do more than gasp and slap a hand against the wall for balance. He maneuvered her quickly, shifting her so that her thighs landed on his shoulders. She cried out in shock, but then there was no more time as he began devouring her.

The possession was as fierce there as it had been in her mouth. Her back was braced against the wall, her bottom held tight by his hands. That left his lips and tongue to do whatever he willed with her. In her. Swirling and thrusting and sucking while her body undulated against the wall.

"Nathan!" He wasn't listening so she reached down and lifted his head by his ears, pulling him away from her so she could breathe. "Nathan!" she said, her hands burrowing into his hair. "Take me." He blinked, obviously not understanding. She so tightened her grip on his hair and spoke as clearly as she knew how. "I don't want your mouth. I want your penis in me now!"

"Tigresses don't—"

She jerked his head to emphasize her point. "Now, Nathan, or I swear I'll kill you." She shifted her legs with a hard jerk so that she tumbled backward. Thank God for the wall or she would have had a painful drop to the floor. As it was, she only managed to get one foot to the floor, her other still hooked on his elbow.

Then she slammed her hands against his shoulders. "I've been dreaming about you since you rented the apartment. I've been wet from the first moment you smiled." She shoved at him again and he tilted back a half inch. "I don't understand your tigress crap. I don't care that you have issues. Right now, I hate you and want you at the very same moment. So choose, buster, are we in a relationship or not? And if so, then you better get naked now."

"Tracy," he began, his voice strangled. "I can't think of anything but you. I can't breathe without wanting you—"

She kissed him. She took his mouth with hers and plundered him while fumbling blindly at the clasp of his jeans. She found it. She opened it. She shoved it down just far enough for his penis to pop free. Then she was holding it, squeezing and pulling and—

He stepped backward, but only to grab her hips and

push her down. She landed on the stairs, which, as far as she was concerned, was the perfect place. But when she looked into his eyes, she saw torment there and a desperate fight against himself. His nostrils were flared, his eyes narrowed and focused, and yet there was something else that held him apart.

"Nathan, just let go." She still held him in her hands so she could feel how he trembled. He was poised between her thighs, his cock so large, so alive, and yet so far away from where she wanted. She arched, trying to draw him closer.

He tightened his grip on her hips, holding her still. "I cannot—I will not lose myself in you. I won't!"

She smiled and touched his lips. "And yet you are still here."

He sobered, his expression turning haunted. "And yet I am still here." He leaned down and touched his forehead to hers. "I couldn't sleep, couldn't eat, couldn't breathe without thinking of you."

"For God's sake, quit being so damn noble!" With a surge of anger, Tracy gripped him with her hands to position him. She tensed, broadening her stance just enough so that—

He was ready for her. As she adjusted, he gripped her torso. As she moved, he switched her momentum such that she fell sideways, off the stairs to the hard entryway floor. "This way," he said.

She wanted to protest. She didn't want sixty-nine on the floor. But it was all he was willing to give, so she took it. His erection swelled right before her eyes. She saw the dark red color, the smooth velvety skin, and the pearl of moisture on the tip. She leaned forward and tasted the salty drop, then heard him groan in hunger.

"Tracy…" he moaned against her thigh. Her name was filled with a reluctant desperation.

She smiled knowing that his need was stronger than his resistance. She slipped her hand down his shaft to explore his balls. He responded by burrowing his face between her knees. His tongue extended to the inside of her thigh, licking and nipping.

She rolled her tongue around his tip again. The taste was as before, but his gasp—that was better. He delved between her folds. She hadn't even felt him move his head, but his tongue was there, thrusting into her. Her body arched in reaction. She was so sensitive. But she would not do this alone.

She engulfed him. Like sucking on a large, thick lollipop, and yet so much more. Life was pulsing in her mouth. It was his energy just like before. Large, primal and very, very male.

He nipped higher on her thigh, but not where she most wanted it. She felt him pause, his lips curving into a smile. "Shall we drink each other, tigress? I will give my power to you. Will you give me yours?"

"I'll give you whatever you want, Nathan, whatever you need." Her tongue toyed with his shaft. She could not resist the energy tingling against her lips. She squeezed his balls, and the energy seemed to tighten. She rolled her tongue around his tip, and the energy swirled along with her motion. And when she began to suck—to stroke with one hand and suck with her mouth, it was as though she concentrated his energy into a laser of pure male light. His power purified for her drinking.

She would have said something. She would have told him how incredible he was. But then he began to stroke her. She felt his tongue thrusting, toying, drinking. Within moments, her orgasm began. She stared to undulate, the internal pump compressing, tightening her energy into wave upon wave of pleasure. But then he put his mouth to her clit and began to suck. Just like with him, her power seemed to follow the pull of his lips. Her orgasm seemed to flow through and down to her clit. He was drawing her energy into him. And she…

She increased her suction. His hips jerked. She could feel his tension, taste the build up of power just behind his organ. He was supposed to stop now. The books said he should stop to conserve his energy, but she would not let him go and he didn't stop himself. She heard him groan, the pull on her clit interrupted as he gasped. His organ seemed to shudder and then he thrust powerfully inside her mouth. Again and again until the beautiful energy that was Nathan began to pour forth. It came in a gushing waterfall. It flew into her mouth, into her body. The white light that was him flowed into her. Nathan: purified and beautiful.

She drank and drank while below, she poured into him. An eternal circle, wondrous and ever flowing.

Divine?

For a moment, yes, she thought she would go to heaven. She felt the circle grow, rising higher and taking them both upward. Flight! But only for a moment.

Then it was gone. She and Nathan lay on the front hallway floor gasping, exhausted, while the echoes of pleasure rippled through her body. Fabulous, and yet not quite divine. Suppressing the disappointment, she smiled and focused on the shimmering aftereffects.

"Now this is the way to spend a Sunday morning," she

murmured. Then she closed her eyes. Tracy felt the rise and fall of his chest, and listened to the thundering beat of her own heart as it slowly steadied. She rolled away from him, only far enough to look into his dazed eyes. He kept a hand on her thigh; and she idly stroked his knee. In another five minutes, she roused herself to speak.

"You're going to have to get over this virginity thing. If I want to have sex with you…" She pressed a kiss onto his thigh. "Real sex, then that's my choice. There's no reason for me to keep my virginity."

He sighed, and she saw regret settle on his features. "I am not protecting you. I am—"

"Keeping yourself from being involved with me?" She pushed up to look pointedly at him. "How's that going for you? If you recall, you broke up with me two days ago and yet here we are."

He looked at her, and she could see him gather his thoughts. Then he pushed up, coming to sit on his knees before her. The motion was fluid and powerful. It was as if he had gone from exhaustion to controlled essence, all in one movement.

She shifted more slowly, pushing upright so that they faced eye to eye.

"The last woman I loved was a white woman like you."

Tracy flinched as a surge of jealousy hit her hard. Her hands were tensed into claws. "I don't really want to know this."

Nathan ignored her, continuing as if she hadn't spoken. "She is white and beautiful, but that is her only similarity to you. She was soft, giving, ultrafeminine whereas you…"

"Are you saying I'm too butch?"

He frowned. "I don't know what that means. I think

you're the strongest woman I've ever met. Smart, determined, and with a great capacity to love. You have built a home for you and your brother. I admire that."

She threw up her hands to cover the embarrassment she felt. She was proud of her accomplishments, but to hear him say it like that... Well, it thrilled her down to her toes. "So I'm awesome. Let's forget this tigress stuff and keep going—"

"You're killing me, Tracy."

She blinked, unsure how to react to that. He appeared serious, but... "You mean that figuratively, right?"

He shrugged. "I was kicked out of the temple because I loved her to the exclusion of all else."

She swallowed, not wanting to think about this other student, but unable to stop herself. "Did you do..." She gestured to the floor. "Did you do that with her, too?"

His shoulders tightened. "Yes. Whenever she allowed me."

"Well, then," she said, disappointment curling in her stomach. "So I'm not special."

He shrugged, his hands lifted in a gesture of helplessness. "You are special. She was special. And I love you completely."

Somehow the words didn't quite thrill her as she'd once thought they would. "You loved them all, didn't you? All your students." She was beginning to understand why he held himself apart from her. "You're trying not to repeat past mistakes. And, to you, I'm just like all of them."

# 15

NATHAN WATCHED THE COLOR drain from Tracy's face. He knew he had just hurt her badly. Just as he knew that he was lying through his teeth. Tracy not special? That was like saying a tsunami was just another storm. Sure there were similarities, but what he had felt for all those other women, all those other tigresses, was nothing compared to what he felt for her now.

Which was why he had to lie to her. She was the same as them in one key respect: she was a tigress. Whether she understood it or not, she was one of the best. She could be a goddess among men. Perhaps he could convince her not to pursue a life at the temple. She was, after all, fully American, fully embedded in U.S. culture. She didn't want to live in a foreign country away from everything she loved.

But she had gone to heaven; she had touched the divine. He had felt her disappointment a moment ago. He'd recognized the sigh that had come just after, the frustration that this orgasm hadn't led to more. Though she had tried to hide it, he had watched for it. He knew she longed for heaven. Her body craved it, and that he would not be able to give it to her. He was not a dragon practitioner anymore. He had given up that life, but he could not deny it to her.

"Perhaps I should make some tea," he said. "Then we can talk."

"You and your tea," she groused, but then relented. "Fine. I'll go get dressed."

"Or perhaps you would prefer a bath?" She did not really seem in the mood to hear what he had to say. "I could bring the tea to you there."

"Or perhaps an omelet?" she asked drily. "And some pancakes while you're at it. How 'bout a whole freaking ten-course meal?" She glared at him but he saw the shimmer of tears in her eyes. "You are the most confusing man I've ever met!" Then she grabbed her clothing and stomped up the stairs.

He watched her go, his eyes lingering on the curve of her bottom, the power in her legs, even the sway of her hips. Yes, bringing out her tigress had strengthened the natural sensuousness of her movements, but he had noticed her even before that evening in his apartment. He had seen the clarity in her eyes, and the simple honesty in her every movement. He never had to guess what she was thinking or what she wanted. Tracy was a woman who decided on her course and did not hesitate. Those traits would serve her well at the temple.

Nathan sighed and pulled on his pants. The power he had drawn from her energized his movements. He had given as much as he had received, and yet the combination somehow left him stronger, better, more balanced. That was how it should be between a man and a woman. As each poured power into the other, they should grow stronger—together.

That was what he thought, but the idea was anathema at the temple. Attachments between people only increased the ties to earthly life. And ties to earth did not help one attain the divine. So his mother said, and so all at the temple believed.

He crossed into the kitchen and began a search for the basics. Tracy joined him a few minutes later. He felt her watching him as he stood at the stove. He was so attuned to her energies that he would know where she was all over the world. Such was the power of this tigress over him.

"You know, for a man who wants to dump me, you're doing everything wrong."

He smiled as he scooped out the omelet and set it on a plate. "I served as cook to the temple for a short time. Then one day, my sister said my dumplings tasted like pig shit. She's been cook ever since."

Tracy looked at the simple food and smiled, her face lighting under the cover of another of her baseball caps. "I'll try to remember that if you ever make me dumplings. As for this… It smells great." She carried it to the table while he began making his own. But then the teakettle whistled. He started to reach for it, but she was there before him, pouring the hot water into mugs. He said nothing as she worked—there was no reason to—and yet his heart clenched nonetheless. She thought nothing of helping him, of pouring her own tea, of waiting to eat until he could join her. He knew of none at the temple who would do such a thing.

*"Bon appétit,"* she quipped when he finally joined her at the table. He smiled, but didn't eat. Instead, he watched her face as she closed her eyes and chewed with appreciation. "Mmm. Definitely better than pig shit," she said. Then she blushed. "Sorry. That was probably inappropriate."

"It was wonderful," he said, unable to express how her

lack of artifice entranced him. Then he took a closer look at her scrubbed face, completely free of makeup. He saw her sexless sweatshirt and baggy pants. "It won't work, you know." She glanced up, startled as he gestured to her hideous clothing. "Dressing so badly. You are a tigress inside. Your sexuality will attract men even if you wear garbage bags. And you will feel the song of desire no matter how tightly you restrain your actions."

She looked at him with a solemn expression. "Then it's a good thing I dress to suit myself." She waved at her clothing. "It's comfortable."

"Then it's a good choice," he answered.

He took a bite of his food, tasting nothing. What would he give up to cook breakfast for her every morning just like this? To hear what she really thought, to feel her appreciation in every bite? How glorious to simply live with her as a man lived with a woman—no games, no ulterior motives, just life without the eternal quest for something beyond?

"Nathan—"

He would give everything he had. But it wasn't his future at stake. It was hers.

"Nathan, you're staring."

"Your brother plays American football, right?"

She blinked. "Um. Yeah, but Nathan—"

"Just answer my questions for a moment, please." He glanced at the team photo on the refrigerator door. "Is he is good at it?"

She smiled. "Yes, he is."

Not surprising. Joey had the build of a football player. "What if you knew he was the best of his age? Possibly— with training—to be the greatest NFL player of all time."

She snorted. "Joey? He's good, but not that good.

With luck, he'll get a scholarship to a division-two school. But—"

"Imagine he was that good, and you knew it, but he didn't. Imagine that you saw a great pro career in front of him, that he could be revered for all time as the best player ever, but he didn't want to do it."

She snorted again and cut a big bite out of her omelet. "Not a chance. Joey loves football. If he were that good, he'd be picking his pro team and what multimillion-dollar car he wanted to buy."

"But what if he didn't understand?" Nathan pressed. "What if he didn't know what being a great football player meant, and he didn't even want to explore it? Maybe he was happy doing whatever he'd been doing before he started to play."

"You mean like being a handyman? He used to love tooling around with Dad doing household repairs and stuff. Male bonding and all that, but boy, did he love it."

Nathan smiled. "Exactly!"

She shrugged. "Where are you going with this?"

"Wouldn't you encourage him to explore football? To see what the possibility was before he decided?"

"Of course, I would." Her eyes softened as she gazed at the photo of her brother. "It's not that I like watching my brother get flattened by a dozen other guys, but he should know his options before he decides on his future. That's why I want him to go to college…." She frowned as she turned back to Nathan. "Where are you going with this?"

He bit his lip, forcing himself to explain though everything inside him urged to keep silent. He was happy teaching her about her energies. But that would be like keeping her in high school when she could be so much, much more.

"You have that capability, Tracy, as a tigress. You could be revered by millions, heaven at your feet. You can—"

"In a cult that no one's ever heard of? Yippee."

He abruptly leaned forward, gripping her hand. Didn't she understand? "You have to go to the temple, Tracy," he said. "You have to know what you're giving up."

She set down her fork, her expression tightening as she spoke. "Is that why you keep pressuring me to go to Hong Kong? To meet with this guy Stephen?" She shook her head. "No way."

His hand tightened painfully then abruptly released. "*I* want nothing of the kind, Tracy. But that's not my place, is it?"

She frowned. "Of course, it is. I mean, if you want to, you know, date me."

His gaze snapped to hers. Didn't she understand how hard this was for him? "So as your boyfriend, I can tell you what to do and where to go? I can keep you from your potential, all because I want you to myself?"

She caught his gaze and held it, her expression intense. "*Is* that what you want?"

He abruptly possessed her mouth. He took her as if he were staking a claim. He pushed himself into her; he arched her back and would have had her on the table in a moment, if he had his way. She had to understand that. So he kissed her without compromise, without give and take, only possession. And then he let her go.

"Is that what you want? I will own you if you like." Then he looked at her. "But first tell me that you do not long for heaven. That you do not wish to return there again."

"You took me there before—"

Nathan shook his head, forced to admit the truth. "Luck. A fluke. But to learn to go there on purpose, you must go to the temple. And Stephen. I can't lead where I've never been."

She stared at him, and he saw the yearning in her eyes. He didn't want to see it, but her longing was undeniable and she knew it. "This is ridiculous!" she snapped. "I'm not NFL material."

He towered over her. "Fine. Deny your potential. Deny what you have experienced and known from the very beginning. But at least admit the truth—you want to return to heaven."

"Yes!" She snapped the word, but then abruptly deflated and her gaze canted away. "Of course, I want to go back there."

He let her words hang in silence. He let her absorb the truth of her desire. And then he delivered the final blow and the real reason he had shown up here this morning. "I leave tomorrow for Hong Kong."

Her eyes leaped back to him. "You're leaving? Now?"

He stepped away from her. If he stood much longer beside her, he would give in and make love to her, but that would ruin everything for her. "You may come with me, if you want. You can visit the temple, talk with my mother, learn what is possible for you." He had no doubt that she would choose to remain in Hong Kong. The tigress in her was too strong to be denied.

"You're going to Hong Kong. Tomorrow. And you want me to go with you." Her voice was flat with shock.

"The situation at home has grown very bad very quickly. My mother is spending recklessly. If she is not stopped now, there will be nothing left for anybody."

She frowned. "But I thought you didn't have anything."

He shook his head. "We have only one thing—the temple. For a hundred years, it is all that we have ever owned." He lifted his gaze to meet her. "I intend to sell it."

"Sell the temple?" She gasped. "But...how? What?"

He shrugged, feeling the weight of his decision. "I can't let my mother continue as she is. She will beggar us in a year. Then we will lose the land anyway."

"So you're going to sell?"

"The temple will remain the same. That is a condition of the sale. Then all the money will be held in trust for my mother, aunt and siblings."

Tracy nodded, her agile mind already understanding more of the financial details than his family ever would. "Is your mother okay with this?"

He tightened his jaw. "She has no choice. She gave me power of attorney long ago." He lifted his chin, embarrassment and pride at war inside him. "Even as a child, I feared this day would come."

"Nathan, I'm so sorry." She reached out to touch his hand. Without thinking, he flipped his hand over so he could grip her palm to palm.

"It doesn't matter," he said. "The temple will survive. My family will have enough to do what they want, and..." He forced his next words out. "I am available as your guide to introduce you to Hong Kong. I can ease your way into the temple."

She narrowed her eyes. "I can't possibly afford a trip to Hong Kong. And neither can you. So where—"

"Stephen has loaned me the money. And he has paid for your ticket—round trip, first class, open-ended return."

She laughed—a short burst of air that filled the room.

"Are you nuts? You think I can go to Hong Kong tomorrow morning?"

He nodded. "I don't think you can resist it."

Tracy studied him, her gaze silent and hard. And the longer she remained quiet, the more his hopes rose. Maybe she did have the strength to resist the siren call of priesthood. Spirit would not influence her, and her scruples would not allow her to accept a free ticket from a man she didn't know. Maybe...

"All right," she said.

His hopes plummeted, but still a tiny sliver of his heart held on. "All right what? You will refuse to go?"

She pushed up from her chair so that she faced him eye to eye. "All right, Nathan, I'll go to Hong Kong with you. My brother can cover for me here. I'll meet this Stephen. I'll see what my big possibilities are for divinity or priestesshood or whatever. But you know what I'll really be doing when I'm there looking at your secret tigress rites?"

Nathan didn't answer. He already knew she would be walking the path of the divine tigresses. He knew that within a week, he would be nothing more than a fond memory, stepping stone along her road.

"I'm going to find out what happened to you, Nathan. I'm going to find out how you can claim to love me, kiss me with such passion, even send me to heaven, and yet still want to throw me to another man. I'm going to learn about the secret life and times of Nathan Gao."

He stared at her, shocked to see that she really did mean exactly what she said. "But I have no secrets. There is nothing for you to find except your own potential."

"Yeah," she drawled. "And I'm Joe Namath reborn."

# 16

THEY LEFT BEFORE DAWN the next morning. It was a miracle that she already had a passport, but with the stricter ID requirements, she'd gotten one last year. Then there was packing and a surprisingly quick discussion with Joey. Far from being upset by her trip, her little brother was thrilled to get the chance to manage the apartment building himself. Tracy could only pray that he remembered he was supposed to go to school, too.

Their flights went from Champaign to Chicago to Los Angeles to Hong Kong. Then there was the endless wait through customs before meeting a limo that wanted to take them directly to Stephen's home. Even though Tracy could barely see straight, she had the strength to flat-out refuse. She and Nathan would go to the tigress temple now. Stephen could visit tomorrow after she'd had a bath, breakfast—or was it dinner?—and felt a little more oriented.

The driver had no choice but to agree, and she had Nathan there to make sure they were driving to the right place. Then she collapsed backward against his outstretched arm and thought she might take a little nap. Except, of course, she had never been out of Illinois, much less the United States. And no matter how tired she felt, she couldn't suppress the excitement zipping down her spine.

She was in Hong Kong! And it was *huge!* Flying in, she had seen mountains and buildings and more buildings. Nathan had told her of huge shopping districts, flea markets and designer boutiques. Of food that ran the gamut from curbside stir fry to $500-a-plate dining.

Tracy had listened closely to everything he'd said. He was her only source of information since there hadn't been time to pick up a guidebook before leaving Illinois. But what struck her most was his description of his native island, Lamma. It turned out that what she called Hong Kong was actually a network of over two hundred islands. Whereas Hong Kong was a steep rocky place of high rise after high rise, Lamma was mostly unspoiled by urban sprawl. In fact, his temple home didn't even have electricity.

The concrete road out of the airport felt busy to her, but Nathan assured her that the traffic was light. As they drove, she caught a glimpse of a massive bronze Buddha and gasped, "Is that your temple?" The statue was huge!

"No," he answered, his voice warm against her cheek. "The tigresses are not so wealthy or as obvious as Po Lin."

She turned and pressed a kiss to his beard-roughened cheek. "Because you study sex? It's important to keep a low profile?" She hadn't forgotten that the Hong Kong police still believed the temple was a glorified prostitution ring.

"Because we use all that our bodies are capable of to launch our way to heaven." He looked down at her, and when she quirked an eyebrow at him, he released a carefree laugh. "And yes, sex is often a hidden discussion among the Chinese."

"Not just among the Chinese," she murmured, her attention drawn back to the landscape. Very soon, Buddha was far away and they were zooming toward the huge skyscape of Hong Kong Island. "How do we get to your home?"

"By ferry then bicycle. Or Stephen's car."

She blinked. "Seriously?" She couldn't imagine a place that she couldn't get to by car. Certainly not in this huge, zooming metropolis. "I think I'm getting whiplash. It's like how I imagine Gotham City on steroids. And yet your home doesn't have electricity."

He began pointing out highlights, talking about things he had done and seen as a child. He'd had footraces against boys on bikes and sometimes won because the road was so rocky. He had carried packages for tourists at Stanley Market for a Hong Kong dollar—less than a U.S. quarter. He had even snuck onto the ferry and ridden for hours….

Then they were at that very same ferry, unloading their luggage to sit on a large open ferry boat. Though there was enough seating for two hundred, barely twenty people shared the ride with them, and no one joined them at the very windy bow. Tracy watched the water and the skyline as long as she could, but in the end, she simply closed her eyes, lifted her face to the wind and felt the warm, strong presence of Nathan as he stood by her side, his arm around her waist, his broad shoulders blocking the worst of the wind.

"Perfect," she said. He couldn't hear her. The wind snatched the word away, but when she opened her eyes she caught him looking down at her, a yearning in his eyes that took her breath away. She would have stretched up on her toes to kiss him then, but he turned away. Still being noble, she supposed, letting her see if she had some great pro-football career. So she pinched him as hard as she could, and when his face snapped back to her, she surged up on her toes and kissed him. "I choose my path," she said a moment later. She spoke right in his ear so he would hear her. "I choose."

He didn't answer. She could tell he didn't believe her. He simply turned away, but the hand that held her waist pulled a little tighter, and she happily snuggled into his side. They stayed like that all the way to the quaint wood pier that led to a well-trod footpath obviously designed for tourists.

Their driver had parked the limo back on Hong Kong Island, then followed them onto the ferry. He now spoke to Nathan in rapid Chinese before grabbing Tracy's suitcase and taking off at a run. She had enough time to gasp before Nathan smiled. "He is going to get the car. We will meet him up at the road."

She looked around at the pristine walking paths, the railings that led to a raised pagoda, and the signs that pointed to a seafood restaurant. Nowhere did she see any cars. A few bicycles, yes. Even rickshaws with smiling runners hoping for fares. But a car? The road wasn't large enough. But she dutifully followed Nathan up a path to a long track of what looked like honeycomb pavement with Bermuda grass poking up everywhere. Then before she could comment on that, the cutest three-wheeled vehicle decorated in zebra stripes appeared. She burst out laughing at the solar panel on top, only to subside into surprise as she climbed inside. It was comfortable, airconditioned and really quite roomy.

"This is Stephen's ZAP car," Nathan said in a bland tone. "He paved the road, as well. Both are very environmentally friendly."

Tracy twisted to look at Nathan. "He paved the road?" She tried to conceive of that much wealth. Of a man who could build a road—miles and miles of it—simply for his convenience. "Just how rich is this Stephen guy?"

Nathan didn't answer as he twisted, straining to see out the left side of the little car. "We will climb a bit now. Five minutes by car, but…" He shook his head, a smile lighting his features. "Forever if you are carrying buckets of water."

"You love this place," she murmured.

"It was my home."

They traveled the rest of the way in silence while a mangrove field sped past. The switchbacks in the road were frighteningly tight, but the beauty was unmistakable—and utterly foreign.

She tucked a little tighter to Nathan's side though one glance at his animated profile reminded her that she was the stranger here, not him. "I don't suppose there's any place to grab a burger here, is there?"

He smiled, his eyes trained ahead. "There will be food at the temple. My sister makes the best tea eggs in all of China."

Tracy remained silent. She hadn't felt hungry so much as out of place. A fast-food burger joint would have given her a welcome sense of familiarity. The promise of tea eggs didn't ease the anxiety knotting her stomach.

Then they arrived. The ZAP car rounded a corner and stopped dead in a brick courtyard before a large, exotic building with clay roof tiles shaped into dragons and tigresses. The walls were painted white except for the two large red columns that flanked a large, red double door. Red banners hung down either side, their gold Chinese characters flowing gently in the breeze.

"I know it is very shabby looking," Nathan said just before the driver opened the car door. "But our fame comes from the beauties within, not the walls without."

She didn't have the words to explain that she found it stunningly beautiful. Only now that she looked did she see peeling paint and the frayed fabric. Then Nathan offered her his hand. She grabbed it like a lifeline as she stepped out into the humid, subtropical air.

She was just meeting his gaze, holding on to the familiarity of his dark eyes and sexy eyebrows when a high squeal cut through the air followed by a rushed flurry of Chinese. Nathan turned immediately, releasing Tracy's hand to wrap a stunningly beautiful woman in his arms. She squealed and cried and spoke all in one breath while Tracy stood to one side and tried to guess who this was. Sister? Lover?

Her age was hard to estimate, but her skin was dewy soft, her hair sleek and jet-black. Was this one of the women Nathan had fallen in love with? Was she a former lover? Tracy tried to suppress a surge of jealousy as Nathan finally unwound the woman's arms and set her back down. Then they both turned to look at her. Tracy forced herself to smile despite the envy biting deep. The woman defined willowy beauty. Looking at her now, Tracy judged her to be forty years old. She wore no makeup, but her eyes were dark, her lips a soft pink and her small body was perfectly accented in a silk skirt and tight bodice.

"Tracy," Nathan said as he smiled warmly at the woman. "This is my aunt Li Li. You may call her Tigress Lily. She speaks no English, but she has a good heart."

Tracy nodded politely, her mind grappling with details.

"Your aunt? But she is so young—", Her words were cut off as the tigress abruptly grabbed Tracy's hand and shook it vigorously. She was all smiles as she gestured inside, her words flowing like a babbling brook.

"She says Stephen told them we were coming, but not when. She is very happy it is so soon, but they did not have enough time to prepare a proper welcome for a new tigress."

"Tell her that I don't need—" Tracy began, but Nathan interrupted.

"Don't bother," he said with a laugh. "She won't stop speaking long enough to hear you. Just smile and follow along."

Tracy had no choice but to agree as she was half dragged inside. The front hallway was dark, but pleasantly cool compared to the outside heat. Tigress Lily kept up a running banter as she led them into a cushioned sitting room. Sparse wood furniture decorated the space, but mostly there were silk cushions everywhere—the floor, the chairs, even on the low coffee table. Lily swatted them aside, then guided Tracy to one of the lower chairs.

Another voice sounded, again in excited Chinese. Nathan turned to the door only to wrap his arms around a girl of maybe sixteen. She was dressed in light cotton, her hair in two long pigtail braids. Her happy smile was more than returned, especially when Nathan pointed out the flour that coated her braids.

"My sister Cai Ting, the chef," he said as the girl jerked her hair out of his hand.

"Hello—" Tracy started only to have the girl bow deeply before her.

"My greetings, Tigress Tracy. We are honored to have you here."

Other voices—all female—came around the corner. She'd thought temples were quiet, holy places, but she was obviously wrong. This was a place of noisy, chattering women all pushing forward to greet Nathan before bowing formally before her. Tracy nodded back, becoming more bewildered as bodies crowded into the small sitting room. And then, almost as if someone had hit a mute button, the room fell abruptly silent.

Tracy had been about to say some greeting, but managed to choke her words off before hers was the only voice in the suddenly hushed room. She looked to Nathan for a clue, but he was surrounded by gorgeous women and was blocked from her view. Then the women began to part, some dropping their heads in respect, some looking with rapt adoration to...

A young Chinese woman of stunning beauty and elegance. In her thirties, she was near the peak of her sexuality. Her body stalked through the air: sleek, supple and entirely predatory. Her face had the dewy softness of youth, but with a lush beauty to her full, moist lips. Her hair fell behind her in a curtain of perfect black silk, and her eyes seemed dark and mysterious, as if she looked upon great secrets of the universe. But it was her body that caught one's attention as it seemed to offer every exotic, erotic delight.

While Tracy stared, Nathan stepped away from his gaggle of women to stand at the beauty's side. "Tracy," he said, "may I present to you the leader of our order, Tigress Mother Pin Ya."

Tracy had the strongest urge to curtsy, but she didn't quite know how. So instead, she dipped her head in greeting, not even bothering to offer her hand. "I am honored to meet you," she said.

The Tigress Mother didn't speak, but her gaze studied Tracy from head to toe, no doubt seeing the wrinkled clothing and the extra pounds on her hips. It was ridiculous that a beautiful woman could make Tracy feel so inferior, but then the woman was extraordinarily beautiful.

Silence reigned for several heartbeats while Tracy struggled not to look to Nathan for help, or worse, bite her lip the way she had as a child. It took another dozen beats before Tracy found her spine. So she wasn't beautiful; she was still a person. Though it took an act of will, Tracy did it. She steeled her shoulders and met the woman's gaze eye to eye, earning an arched eyebrow as her reward.

Meanwhile, Nathan began speaking. His words were in Chinese, so Tracy understood none of it except for one word: *Mama.*

The woman flicked his comments away with a negligent wave, somehow managing to make even that gesture a sensuous delight. And then a brain cell managed to fire. Understanding slipped through until Tracy's gaze shot to Nathan. *"Mama,"* she echoed. "You said Mama. This can't be your mother."

Nathan nodded. "I told you my mother led the temple."

"Yes, but… But… She's so young!"

The Tigress Mother smiled, the gentle pull of her lips bowing her mouth in a most feminine display. "How old do you think I am, little cub?" she asked in English. Her voice was velvety smooth, her accent almost negligible.

Tracy swallowed, scrambling to upgrade her estimate. "Um, forty?" But that would mean she'd had Nathan when she was eleven.

"I turned fifty-eight this year."

Tracy swallowed her knee-jerk "bull hockey," response. Instead, she simply shook her head. No plastic surgeon was that good. This simply could not be Nathan's mother. Meanwhile, the Tigress Mother gestured about the room, her wave going first to Nathan's aunt.

"Tigress Lily is fifty-four," she said. Tracy gaped.

"Tigress Ting Bo is forty-eight," she continued. Then one by one, other tigresses stepped forward, each announcing their ages with clear pride.

"Seventy-one."

"Thirty-four."

"Twenty-two."

All appeared younger than their stated ages, some by a little, some by staggering amounts. But none could match the apparent youth or sensuality of the Tigress Mother.

"And you, Tigress Tracy," she asked after a half dozen had spoken, "what is your calendar age?"

"Twenty-five," she answered, her voice tiny.

"Ah, the same age as my daughter," she said as the flour-dusted girl stepped in. The one who looked sixteen.

Cai Ting grimaced. "Mother, please. She has come all the way from the United States, and we haven't even given her tea. Let her get her bearings."

"Of course," Mother Tigress said with a bow. Then she settled herself into the largest, most ornately carved black lacquer chair. A queen in her throne? It would be easy enough to think so, and yet as she sat there, she appeared not so much a queen as a courtesan—gorgeous, sensuous, her every breath an act of mysterious seduction. Then her eyes scanned the crowd. "Attend to your studies," she said sweetly.

The room quickly emptied of all except for Tracy, Nathan and his mother.

"My brother is at work," he said. "You'll meet him tonight."

Tracy nodded, completely fine with slowing the introductions. "Is there a room where I could freshen up?" she asked. "And where did my luggage go?"

"Nathan will take it to Dragon Stephen's practice room," the Tigress Mother answered. "There is a bathing chamber there."

Tracy opened her mouth to object. She had no intention of practicing anything with anyone just yet. But before she could respond, another gorgeous woman entered the room. She was carrying a silver English tea tray, which she settled carefully—and of course beautifully—upon the low coffee table. In truth, she appeared nothing less, nothing more than anyone else Tracy had met so far—young, beautiful and with a sensuous quality about her that could not be denied.

The difference? She was white. A redhead to be exact, complete with freckles and emerald-green eyes. And as soon as she set the tea tray down, she looked up at Nathan and offered him a full, seductive smile. She said something in Chinese—a greeting no doubt—her voice a husky whisper that felt like claws down Tracy's spine.

It wasn't, of course, but Tracy felt her hatred rise even before Nathan's gaze shuttered closed. Obviously this was the last woman he'd been with. The lover who was just like Tracy, except… Except Nathan did not look even warmly at that woman. He bowed politely to her, then turned to his mother. "I will see to the luggage."

Tracy was so busy feeling a catty satisfaction at his

coldness to the redhead that she missed his words until he exited the room. He was leaving? Abandoning her to his mother and the Irish sea witch?

"Nathan?" She half rose out of her seat, but was stopped by a firm hand on her shoulder. It was the Tigress Mother, pressing her back into her seat. Damn, her hand was strong. Tracy could have fought it off, but politeness kept her from being rude to an elder—no matter how young the woman seemed. Meanwhile, Nathan paused long enough in the archway to send her a wan smile.

"I'll be in the kitchen with my sister. It is not far." Then he glanced at his mother. "And you should get to know the head of your order."

"But…" she began, unsure what she was going to say.

"He is quite correct," his mother interposed. Her voice was low, almost like a purr, but with a cutting edge to it that grated on Tracy's nerves. "We must speak to one another as tigresses. No man, not even a tigress's son, can interfere with that."

Nathan took the hint. He was dismissed, and so he bowed to his mother and Tracy—completely ignoring the redhead—and then disappeared. Which left Tracy alone to brave the tigresses in their den, so to speak.

She started with the redhead, turning to inspect the woman with a benign smile. Beautiful, of course. Willowy, like everybody else. But there was an emptiness in the woman's eyes that made Tracy pity her, not hate her. The thought was startling enough that she lost whatever mild greeting she was going to voice. Then the moment was gone as the woman pushed to her feet, bowed reverently to the Tigress Mother and left, as well. Perhaps to run panting after Nathan?

Which left Tracy alone with Nathan's mother. Except turning to the woman, Tracy couldn't think of her as a mother. She was a model, a queen and a tigress, all rolled into one. Tracy mustered a semblance of a smile just as the Tigress Mother released a soft, sensuous sigh.

"Please. The tea is designed to soothe one's nerves after a long journey."

Tracy nodded slowly, looking at the tea tray, and finally got the hint. Apparently, the Tigress Mother wanted her to serve. But tea service hadn't been taught in her high school. She would probably do it all wrong. And wasn't the hostess supposed to serve? Unless this was some weird Chinese custom. Either way, the Tigress Mother was waiting for Tracy to move.

She dutifully shifted to the coffee table. Of course, the only way to settle at the right height was to drop down onto her knees. She did, thankful that her joints didn't pop as they sometimes did. Then she did her best to pour scalding liquid into tiny cups without splashing or spilling. She was just at the most delicate moment when the Tigress Mother spoke.

"Explain to me the sex you have had with my son, and its effect upon you."

She didn't spill. A minor miracle, that. As it was, she carefully set down the teapot to blink stupidly at Nathan's mother.

"He has told me that you visited the Chamber of a Thousand Swinging Lanterns."

Tracy swallowed and nodded.

"Describe it to me."

Tracy opened her mouth, but no sound came out. In the end, she simply closed her eyes, shook her head and lied. "I cannot," she whispered. "I can hardly remember it."

The Tigress Mother narrowed her eyes, and her lips curled in disgust. Tracy had never actually seen a person's lips do that, but curl they did and with utter disdain. "A tigress does not lie," she said. "Not to herself and certainly not to me. Do you wish to be beautiful? Do you wish to look like me when you are sixty?"

"Of course," Tracy answered.

"You have much to learn." She pursed her mouth in a sweet pout. "Stephen can do the initial testing. I fear my son's mind has not been on his studies." She leaned forward, taking one of the teacups with an elegant sweep of her hand. "But he has a knack for finding white tigresses. Sandy was his discovery."

The redhead, Tracy guessed.

The woman's gaze abruptly sharpened. "You wish to return to heaven?"

Tracy looked down at her cup. She didn't want to admit it, but yes, she did. Very much so.

"You will begin with Stephen. He knows how to coax a tigress to dance better than any dragon alive."

Tracy lifted her head. "But I don't wish to study with him. I like my current partner."

The Tigress Mother released a throaty purr of laughter. "You are young, little cub. In this you will be guided by me. My son is not staying." She pushed to her feet. "He needs to study, and I believe your dragon arrives."

The electric ZAP car did not make an engine noise, but the crunch of wheels on brick was unmistakable and surprisingly loud in this busy place. Tracy's gaze leaped to the window, but she couldn't see anything through the wood lattice. Then she looked back to the Tigress Mother, only to realize that the woman had left.

# *17*

STEPHEN CHU WAS NOT handsome. He was too masculine to be labeled anything that soft. He was also dressed in Armani and carried a dozen roses for Tracy. The bouquet of orchids went to the Tigress Mother, passed off reverently as the woman padded away down the hallway.

Then it was Tracy alone again, this time with a ruggedly sculpted Chinese aristocrat, if such things existed in modern China. He stepped forward, offering her the roses. She took them slowly, her smile uncertain. His smile was equally hesitant, but oh so much more charming.

"Miss Williams," he murmured with a slight bow. "I am so pleased to finally meet you." His words sent a low thrill down her spine. He knew just how to modulate his voice to the perfect mixture of friendliness and sexuality.

Tracy blinked, unsure how to react. In truth, the man was perfect. The roses were perfect. The entire rustic setting was perfect for a romantic first meeting. But she didn't want to be attracted to him.

"I had hoped you would come to my home first. I would have let you rest, freshen up, get settled before meeting the Tigress Mother. She can be a bit overwhelming, can't she?" His expression invited her to confide in him. When she didn't say anything, he continued with smooth charm.

"But no matter. The worst is over now. Everything will get better and beyond better soon enough."

"Uh, yeah," she said. "About that…" Her voice trailed away as he waited patiently for her to finish. But she didn't know what to say. "I…uh…"

"You are confused and overwhelmed. Yesterday you were in Illinois where all made sense. And today…" He stepped forward and gently touched her cheek. It was a familiar gesture, but one she didn't step away from. And where their skin touched, a tingling began that heated her face. "Today is the beginning of something very different. I understand, Tigress Tracy. I will wait until you are ready. I am just so pleased that you are finally here at the temple."

She blinked, her words—her thoughts—abruptly blank. He was that suave. And while she stood there looking at him, a student entered the hallway. The woman glanced coyly at Stephen, her manner obviously flirtatious, and Tracy was abruptly surprised by a surge of anger. Stephen was here for her!

Tracy blinked. Except she wasn't interested in Stephen.

She glanced back at the handsome man, seeing wealth and sophistication in his every breath. Better yet, he barely even noticed the other woman. His focus remained completely on her, and she smiled with feminine satisfaction. No, not feminine—feline. Feline satisfaction so strong she almost purred. So this was how the tigresses got their name. What she felt at this moment was very primal, very animalistic, and yes, very, very catty.

Tracy lifted the roses in her arms and all but shoved them at the other girl. "Can you put these in water please?" she asked, not giving the woman a choice. Then she turned back to Stephen. "Perhaps it would have been better to rest before meeting the Tigress Mother. She is a bit more than I expected."

He grinned. "My first meeting with her was horrible. I spilled the tea all over my pants and she had me stand around in my underwear while they were cleaned."

Tracy felt her eyebrows rise. "How old were you?"

He shrugged. "Fifteen. She was my, um, birthday present from my father."

It took a moment for her to understand exactly what kind of present he meant. "Must have been some kind of birthday," she drawled.

Stephen's mouth curved into a slow, seductive smile. "Oooooooh, yeah."

Tracy was equal parts intrigued and shocked. Who gave a tigress to a teenage boy? But before she could speak, he focused all his very potent attention back on her.

"Do you want to clean up before dinner? My chef has prepared the most perfect American meal for you, but there will be Chinese delicacies, as well. Anything your heart desires—"

"Whoa!" Tracy said, holding up her hand. "Your chef?"

He looked charmingly befuddled. "Of course. A new tigress is something to celebrate," he murmured.

Tracy looked at him, trying to sort through her conflicting thoughts. There was little air in the narrow hallway, so she could smell the man's cologne clearly. It was dark, carnal, and…and perhaps it wasn't cologne after all. It was his own scent—as strongly masculine as the Tigress Mother's femininity. And damn if Tracy didn't feel a moistening deep in her core. She didn't want to be interested in this man. She didn't want to be charmed by his good looks, his obvious money, and most of all, the way he set her at ease. But she was charmed. She was also curious. Did he kiss like Nathan? Were all dragons this magnetic?

She lifted her gaze to his and without conscious decision, she licked her lips in enticement. His eyes widened and his nostrils flared. Tracy had a split second to be shocked by her own behavior before Stephen closed the distance between their mouths.

He kissed her. He pressed his mouth to hers, teasing her with his lips, stroking her with his tongue, and yes, he did those same little nips that Nathan did. But Stephen had his own style—more possessive, more demanding. He took what he wanted from her lips, silently daring her to match his fervor taste for taste.

She didn't refuse. She wanted to. Her thoughts were on Nathan, and yet her body was running the show. She returned the kiss, her inner tigress roaring to life as she abruptly shoved her hands in his hair and held him close. They were fused—mouth-to-mouth—fighting, eating, consuming one another without thought as to where they were or what they were doing. It was an act of the body devoid of mind, and yet it was so powerfully primal that she didn't stop.

His hands were on her shirt, and if it had been a blouse, she was sure it would have been on the floor. But she was wearing a collared T-shirt, the one with her brother's high-school name embroidered on the front, and it would not come off without being stripped over her head. Which meant they had to stop kissing. Which meant...

She broke away, jerking her shirt from his hands. Tracy stumbled backward, her breath coming in gasps. Gawd, they were in the hallway! And she had been a breath away from mating on the floor with him!

He swallowed and drew a shaky hand across his mouth. "My God," he whispered. "You are incredible!"

She shook her head, not even knowing what she meant by it.

"It's true then," he continued. "You are a virgin. You must be. No one has—"

"Stop it! Just stop it!" she gasped.

Stephen swallowed and slowly straightened. He smoothed out his tie, readjusted his pants. She could see the bulge there despite the perfect tailoring. He was shaken, his movements betraying an anxiety she guessed he rarely showed. But in his eyes she saw an insatiable hunger—dark and predatory. It scared the hell out of her. Not because he so obviously wanted her, but because she felt an answering cry inside her. The lust had nothing to do with her mind, but everything to do with power calling to power—male energy reaching for female—and she hated it.

"I don't even know you," she panted.

"Tigress training is not about knowing one another," he answered, his voice slowly readjusting from a husky rasp back to smoother, more cultured tones. "It is about power mixing, mating and—"

"Heaven. Yeah, I know. I've been there."

"And you can go back," he coaxed, stepping up before her again. Thankfully, he didn't touch her. "With me, we can both go back to heaven many times. This I know." He took a deep breath. "The hardest part will be keeping your virginity intact. That must be the reason you are so strong."

"No." She forced the words out quickly before she changed her mind. "I'm not an animal. No offense, but it's not what I want. It's strong, really strong, but I'm not a beast to be controlled by lust." She looked up at him and saw him staring at her in dumbfounded shock. Then he closed his mouth, bowing his head slightly in acknowledgment.

"I forgot you are new to this. Such power…" He shook his head. "You are quite right. We must first get to know each other. Talk. You can attend some classes. Then we will speak again."

She was tempted. Lord, how she was tempted. But primal power without emotion? Without a mind guiding it? "No," she repeated. "I… I'm not doing any of this."

He nodded, his eyes canted down. "As you wish," he said. His tone and body posture said he was bowing to her wishes, but Tracy knew it was a lie. He was waiting, stalking, biding his time until the right moment to strike. And God help her, her belly tightened at the thought. Stalked by a rich, handsome man? How awesome was that?

"I…I think I'm going to the kitchen now. I think I need something to eat."

He nodded again. "An excellent idea. And I shall find Nathan. He and I have some business to discuss."

Tracy felt her breath trap in her chest. "Business?"

"Nothing important. I'm sure you have enough to handle right now without trying to sort through the complex financial matters of the temple."

In other words, she shouldn't worry her pretty head about it. Of course, he was right. She had no business poking her nose into their finances. Still, she stayed in the hallway, shifting awkwardly from foot to foot as she tried to make sense of her thoroughly alien environment. "Nathan never mentioned anything about you and the business side of the temple."

Stephen shrugged. "I support the temple in a variety

of ways. Up until now, my financial support has been relatively modest."

She frowned, looking outside. "I thought you built the road up here."

He shrugged. "A calculated risk."

"I see." She did, actually. Or guessed she did. "You're the one buying the temple, aren't you?"

His gaze sharpened with a gleam that had nothing to do with sex. Suddenly his smile shifted to a more professional competence that was even more devastating because it showed total confidence and a glint of pride. "I've waited a long time for this opportunity. I will ensure that the temple survives for another hundred years."

She wanted to find out more. She wanted to know his plans for Nathan's family. But in the end, she shook her head. "I'm sure I'll learn more in time. Right now, I would like to go to the kitchen." And Nathan. She wanted to see Nathan.

Stephen nodded, but he didn't move. Instead, he hesitated. When he finally spoke, his voice was low as if he was confiding in her. "He does not love you, you know. Not how you think. Not forever, not the marrying kind of love."

She gasped, startled by his words. How could he know she was thinking about Nathan?

He reached out and touched her arm. She felt the tingle there, of power arching from him into her. "A man knows when a woman is thinking of another man. But Nathan is a dragon, and we do not love that way."

She stepped backward, trying to find clarity in her thoughts. But that would take more than just distance from this charismatic man. "I thought Nathan was kicked out of the temple."

Stephen shrugged. "He was. His mother did not like him controlling her spending. But that has nothing to do with his training. He was trained as a dragon, trained as someone who touches women and moves on." He shook his head sadly. "Nathan is in a difficult place. He had no example of marriage, normal love. He does not know his father, never heard of weddings until he was ten. He trained since birth to touch a woman and then move on."

"He says he is not a dragon," she said.

"His natural inclination is to attach too easily. This traps him in a place between—too flighty for marriage, but too attached to earth to attain heaven."

"That's not true," Tracy said. "Nathan's very stable. He's taking care of his family, studying to get a good degree." A list of his many admirable qualities formed in her mind while Stephen rocked back on his heels.

"Do not fall for him, Tracy. He is not your future."

She folded her arms across her chest. Everything was happening too fast. She had wanted to learn more about Nathan's family, not plunge headlong into temple politics. But then again, perhaps they were one and the same. Meanwhile, Stephen did not ease up his campaign to win her.

"Every tigress, every dragon must choose between earth or heaven," he said. Then he touched her face, skating a finger over her lips. "Choose heaven and I can give you everything you want." He let his hand drop away. "Choose earth and we will have no more to discuss."

She bit her lip, finally understanding what she had been missing. "Nathan chose earth. That's why he says he's not a dragon. He chose to manage things here on earth."

Stephen shrugged. "Someone has to make sure the

bills are paid, the food is cooked. There is great honor in that path."

"But it is not a dragon's path?"

Stephen's smile grew sensuous, and his entire demeanor shifted into that dark, primal place that called to her on an animalistic level. "I *am* the dragon path," he said.

She swallowed, her options crystal clear: Stephen or Nathan. Except according to Stephen, Nathan was too flighty to be a real life mate on earth. "You're a persuasive man, Mr. Chu. You make it sound like you're my only choice."

"Don't you long to return to heaven?" he pressed. "I can take you there. Again and again, we can both dance with immortals."

She was tempted. The urge to run with Stephen was like a mythical call. But she was more than just her sexual side, and she would not make a decision like this without thought.

"Nathan said he'd be in the kitchen," she said. "Can you show me where that is?"

"Over here," he said in a normal voice. His sexuality abruptly masked beneath his smooth, urbane, ultrarich persona, Stephen escorted her to the largest kitchen she had ever seen.

Tracy stepped inside and was hit by the delightful scents of soy sauce, spicy pork and herbs. Heat crackled across her face, but her attention was on scanning the huge room. She saw movement everywhere: people chopping or stirring or steaming things along a huge wood table or by an equally huge stove. Gleaming pots cluttered her vision, and strange roots dangled from the ceiling. But in all that, she focused on one person: Nathan. He sat at a large wood table and sipped tea. A dumpling lay half-eaten on a plate before him.

Their eyes met immediately, and then his gaze flickered to Stephen right behind her. She stepped forward, wanting Nathan's attention to return to her. It didn't. In fact, he seemed to carefully avoid her as he stood up from his seat.

"Ready now?" Nathan asked.

"If you are," Stephen answered.

"I am."

"Then, shall we?"

Nathan nodded and grabbed his battered attaché from the floor. Seconds later, both men had left the kitchen without one more glance at Tracy. She watched them go, still hoping for a connection with Nathan. A look, a touch, anything to remind her that he was still the same Nathan who had carried her into her bedroom, who had served her an omelet and kissed her senseless. But there was nothing.

"He can't see you anymore," said a woman from behind her.

Tracy spun around to see Nathan's sister standing by the table. "What?"

"Nathan. He's handed you over to your new partner. Since he's not part of the temple anymore, he can't talk to you. He's only allowed in the kitchens and back gardens, and that's just because he's family."

Tracy swallowed. "That's silly. He's taught me everything." And she felt lost without him.

Cai Ting gave her a wry smile. "That's exactly why. Do you honestly think you're the first tigress to fall for her teacher? Trust me, it's better this way. Break ties. Move on. Easier for everyone." Then she leaned forward, her expression abruptly fierce. "Better for him."

Tracy swallowed, realizing that everyone here, most especially Nathan, expected her to embrace this tigress training, toss aside everything she knew and abruptly walk into the land of the divine. It couldn't be that simple. It sure as hell didn't feel that easy. And yet, the thought of returning to that heavenly place tempted her. Not to mention the youthful gorgeousness gifted to full tigresses. If Stephen could get her there—and he obviously had as much skill as Nathan—then shouldn't she consider what they suggested? She bit her lip, feeling confused and disoriented.

Cai Ting shook her head. "You need a break. Here, Nathan had me get something for you."

Tracy followed the woman to the table and a covered dish. A moment later, Cai Ting lifted off the lid, and Tracy's heart melted in a rush. Nathan had ordered this for her? With a grin, she grabbed hold of the biggest and best burger she'd ever had in her life.

TRACY OPENED HER EYES to the deepest darkness she'd ever experienced. She tensed, her mind grappling with sensations too rapid to catalog. She was naked and blind. And not alone.

"It's me," came a soft, familiar voice. "It's Nathan. I'm sorry I woke you."

She exhaled in relief, her body sagging into a large comfortable bed. But she was still blind. Her eyes were open, but there was no electricity in the temple and no moon tonight. She might as well have been in a cave, except that she was warm and the silence was comforting, especially with Nathan there…somewhere.

"What time is it?"

"After two in the morning."

"Really? It feels like later." Sleep was rapidly fading as she sat up.

"It's after noon back home."

Of course. Jet lag. "Where are you?"

"Right here." She felt the mattress dip by her feet as he settled on the bed.

"I should be annoyed at you for abandoning me."

"It's the rules, Tracy. I shouldn't even be here now, but I..."

"Had to see me?" She couldn't keep the hope from her voice.

"How was your first day?" he asked, obviously avoiding her question.

"Gorgeous women, ancient texts, frank discussions of sex with your mother." She sighed with dramatic intent. "You know. The usual."

"Of course," he said, humor lacing his tone. She felt the mattress shift as he leaned back against the head-board. "And did you enjoy the usual?"

She hesitated, trying to frame her thoughts. "I got a bunch of stuff on how to control the tigress in me. At least now I'm not so afraid I will jump the next male body I see."

"You never would have. Your strength of will is very disciplined."

"Oh," she teased, "you say that to all us tigress girls." Then she sobered, realizing that he may have said exactly that to other girls. She felt the mattress shift again as he stood, and she abruptly reached out. "Nathan?"

She felt a soft kiss flutter across her cheeks. "Good night, tigress."

"Nathan!" she called again. But she couldn't say it loudly for fear that someone else would hear. And within another breath, she knew he was gone. She collapsed backward on the bed in a huff. Then she heard him, a

voice from the hallway, whispering such that she could
barely catch the words.

"Yes, I had to see you."

SHE WAS AWAKE WHEN he came the next night. She'd been
waiting for him, dozing fitfully, alert for the slightest
sound. She'd already leaped upright when one of the
temple cats had meowed in the hallway. But this time she
knew it wasn't a false alarm. She knew he was there,
standing in the darkness looking at her, though how he
could see anything was beyond her.

"You are awake," he said, his voice a warm jolt of
electricity to her spine. If she hadn't been alert before,
she was now.

"I didn't see you today," she said as she sat up in bed.

"The temple finances are a disaster," he answered as
he moved into her room. "How my mother can mess
things up so quickly is beyond me. She only had a few
months, but…"

"Big debt?"

"Big ignorance. She simply doesn't want to understand anything mortal. Her whole focus is the divine, and
as such, it is our duty to support her in her quest."

"You mean *your* duty." She wrapped her hands
around her knees.

He was silent for a long moment, but then she heard
him step closer. "It is my duty as—"

"Yeah, yeah, oldest male. Embrace the responsibility.
I understand that Nathan, I really do. I just feel bad
because it obviously wears on you."

Tracy felt the mattress dip and smiled. He was going
to stay for a bit. She'd set a candle on the bedside table

and now lit it with unsteady hands. A warm glow filled the chamber, and she was able to finally see him sitting in his wrinkled suit. The light was gentle enough to emphasize his beauty, but she also saw the weariness in his face and the droop in his shoulders.

"You're tired," she said. "Did you get anything to eat?"

He nodded. "My sister left food for me. But what of your day? Temple accounting cannot be nearly as interesting as your first full day as a tigress."

"Doubtful." Today had been a day for Stephen to show off his many accomplishments. Under the guise of "orienting her to Hong Kong," she had wandered the finest boutiques where he had bought her silk robes and sexy lingerie. She had dined in a floating restaurant and then had high tea at the Mandarin hotel. Nathan knew, of course. One of the first things she'd discovered was that she was big news in this little community of women. "You didn't tell me Stephen was that rich. I mean, wealthy, yes, but über-rich? Top-twenty-in-the-world rich?"

His gaze slanted down to the silk coverlet. "Money is nothing to him. He can put you and your brother through college and think nothing of it. He could set you up with diamonds, cars, a villa of your own. Whatever you want, Stephen can give it all to you."

"I don't want material things." She saw him arch a brow at her, and she had the grace to blush. "Okay, okay, so I like the money. I'm human. And frankly, nobody is more surprised than me. But all I want is a financial cushion. I don't need a whole pillow factory."

He frowned at her, and she knew she wasn't making any sense.

"I want enough wealth to live comfortably. I don't need über-wealth."

"And heaven?" he pressed.

And right there was the problem. Every moment she was with Stephen—no matter what he did or what he said—there was something elemental in her attraction to him. His energies, her energies—they yearned toward one another. It didn't help that deep down, she kinda liked the guy. He was unfailingly suave. And who wouldn't love being wined and dined by a gazillionaire?

"There's nothing between us," she said as much to herself as to Nathan. "Chemistry, yes. But a connection? No."

"That makes it easier to launch to heaven, Tracy. Earthly attachments—"

"I know." She'd already heard it from everyone. One couldn't focus on the divine when your mind—or your heart—was on your partner. "Nathan—"

"It will get easier, Tracy. Give it time." Was there a flash of regret in his eyes? She couldn't tell in the dim candlelight. And worse, he was already standing up to leave.

"Don't go, Nathan. Stay and talk to me. Tell me about the sale of the temple."

He paused, his eyes warming into friendship. "What have you heard?"

"Nothing. Honest." She shifted, crossing her legs as she faced him. "So what do you think Mr. I'm-so-rich-I-can't-think-of-enough-ways-to-spend-it is going to do with the temple?"

"Keep it exactly the same or so it says in the contract," answered Nathan softly. "I had hoped that Mama would take on some responsibility after I left. That she would see…"

"I doubt finances are your mother's forte," Tracy said

drily. The Tigress Mother seemed to float through her days and nights, seeing only what she wanted to see, then ignoring all the rest for others to handle. Others like Nathan and his siblings.

"No," he said with clear regret. "Managing money has never interested her."

"So what are you going to do?"

He sighed. "Alienate my mother forever." He reached out and gripped her hand, his warmth enveloping her. "The money will be evenly divided. We all will have plenty to live on assuming it is spent wisely."

And there, of course, was the problem. "Will your mother spend wisely?"

He grimaced. "She will have to. She has destroyed her credit rating. So now, her monthly allowance will be given on a debit card. As long as she remains at the temple, her daily needs will be cared for. That, too, is part of the contract."

Tracy smiled. "You've done well, you know. You've seen to everything and everyone fairly." Then she sighed, guessing at the future. "She's going to hate you for this, isn't she?"

He shrugged. "That, too, sometimes is the lot of the eldest son." He spoke casually, but she knew this wasn't easy for him. She squeezed his hand and saw his expression tighten on his face. It was so intense, she felt as if he were actually touching her cheek, stroking her lips. Her belly tightened; her breath quickened. She had already consumed the yin-dampening tea, done her nightly meditation on *not* being horny. She'd done all the things she needed to so that she would *not* jump the nearest man.

But the nearest man was Nathan. And at the moment,

she wanted nothing more than to touch him, to give comfort, to… She swallowed, realizing the truth in that moment. She wanted to give him the love he had been denied throughout his childhood. But the moment she leaned for him, he leaped out of bed, breaking the connection of their hands.

"You're tired, Tracy. And I shouldn't even be in this part of the temple."

"I'm not tired!" she cried. "And you're here. Please, Nathan, don't go."

She should have saved her breath. He shook his head and crossed quickly to the door. "You're a tigress now, Tracy. You cannot see what is possible with me blocking the view," he whispered. Then he ducked into the hallway.

"Nathan, wait!" She was already dragging on a robe. Then she grabbed the candle and rushed to her door. But by the time she got there, the only living thing in the hall was another temple cat.

# *18*

HE SHOULD LET HER SLEEP. Nathan knew that Tracy had begun classes today. Few people understood the rigorous physical demands put on a tigress. Eternal youth and beauty had to be nurtured every day, and she would be sore and exhausted from her physical studies. He should let her sleep…but he couldn't leave without saying goodbye.

He slipped into her room, inhaling deeply. Her scent filled his mind as it had filled his thoughts from the moment he'd first met her. It was clearer here than in Illinois. Here, she had no access to her perfumes; the air was not purified and circulated as in the United States, and most of all, his mother would have demanded that she throw out any lotions or deodorant.

So now when he saw her lying so sweet in her bed, he could inhale deeply and know that a tigress rested here. That a woman of extraordinary beauty and skill tempted men from this boudoir, and that he was privileged to enter. He smiled as he stepped to her bedside. He had already known that. He had seen her incredible potential long before his mother had begun feeding her purifying teas and food laced with aphrodisiacs.

He set his candle on her bedside table, right next to the one she kept there in case he visited. She lay twisted in the sheets, her body completely naked. He could see the lush mound of one breast, the rounded curve of her hip and the silky bronze coil of her hair about the pillow.

His belly tightened and his organ stretched for her, but he held back. She was not his. Now that she was learning what was possible, he would not remain long at her side. Her destiny was as a tigress. His was...not here. He would be better served to cut ties now. He extended his hand, needing to feel the dewy softness of her cheek, to touch the wet fullness of her lips. How he longed...

She gasped and her eyes fluttered. He drew back instantly, but she had already seen him, and he smiled to see her lips curve in delight. "I didn't mean to wake you," he lied.

"It's all right. I was waiting for you."

He settled gingerly down on the bed beside her. She made room for him, then gasped in pain as she tried to sit up. He reached out to help her, but she had already collapsed back into her pillow with a groan.

"Sore?" he asked.

She cracked an eye at him. "Who knew tigresses did killer yoga?" She wrinkled her nose and began to imitate his mother in her teaching mode. "Tigresses, twist your tail upright! Tigresses, clean your paws! Tigresses, contort your anatomy in ways that aren't humanly possible!"

He chuckled. She had Mama's intonation perfectly. "It is possible, you know," he said. "The willow waist of a tigress is prized by all men." The thought of Tracy with her sparkling eyes and curly hair moving with the supple seduction of a tigress made him break out in a cold sweat. "You will be a magnificent tigress."

"That, or a crippled one. Your mother actually thinks

I'll be able to get my ankles behind my neck. That I'll back-bend like...well, like she does it with that pulsing thing she does with her pelvis. I swear, your mother is incredible!"

His heart plummeted at her words. Tracy was already well on her way to worshipping his mother. "She is a great tigress," he said in a neutral tone. "Would you like me to massage your legs? I know just how. I have done it for my mother and her students for years."

She tensed, her eyes widening at the thought. Then she licked her lips. It was an unconscious movement, and yet it was also the gesture of a tigress. He looked away rather than see the familiar steps of a cub just learning how to seduce.

He pushed off the bed, unaccountably annoyed. He did not want to speak to a tigress right then. "I must go, Tracy. I only came here to—"

She practically leaped out of bed, and her hand latched on his arm. "No, wait! Of course I'd love a massage, but that's not what I was thinking." She paused, biting her lip in nervousness. Oddly enough, the sight reassured him. She was not a fully confident tigress yet. "I...um...I heard the argument. I know you told your family about selling the building. How are you doing?"

Of course she'd heard. He had hoped that her classes would have kept her preoccupied, but the temple was a small place. And his mother had a loud voice when she chose to exercise it.

"I am fine. But I will be leaving in the morning."

Tracy sighed. "Maybe she'll change her mind. She doesn't really intend to disown you, does she?"

He smiled. "She will not recant something spoken so loudly." He swallowed. "I am disowned. Any status I once had at this temple is gone. Even Stephen cannot change that. Mama has absolute control over the religious matters."

"But that's not fair! She—"

Nathan stopped her words with a touch on her leg. She lay under the cover, but he knew she would feel it. And once touching, he could not resist stroking, even through the blanket. "My mother has decided, and I will leave in the morning." Then he took a breath. "This should not affect your training. In truth it will be to your benefit since you are partnered with the new owner. Stephen will see that you don't suffer from my disgrace."

"There wasn't any disgrace," she snapped. "Or at least not yours. What she's doing is—"

"Enough," he responded firmly, though her passionate defense of him warmed his heart. "My siblings and I now have enough money to pursue whatever future we want. My aunt will have an independence she never imagined. And you…" He swallowed. "You are impressing all your teachers with your abilities."

She frowned. "I haven't done anything but talk about sex and try to do yoga that wasn't designed for an American body."

"You are doing very well," he repeated firmly. Then he looked at her, unable to simply leave. One last caress. One last memory. Soon, she would become like all the others. "Let me massage you, Tracy. It can help with the pain—"

She let out a short burst of laughter. "Your family was just ripped apart, and you're here offering to give me a massage. I don't know whether you're the sweetest guy ever or in total denial."

He smiled. He had already worked his hand under the cover enough to finally—blessedly—touch her smooth, porcelain skin. "You are so American sometimes, it makes me smile."

She blinked. "Sorry?"

"A tigress would consider it her privilege to be worshipped by my hands. To be massaged and stroked and—"

"I got it!" she said, and to his shock, a blush stained her cheeks. "I...um...I don't think it's as much a tigress's privilege as the kind of thing she spends her day doing." She leaned forward, her voice dropping to a low murmur that slipped into his blood like a drug. "I had a two-hour class in how to prolong orgasm. Two hours, Nathan. And then we were supposed to experiment on our own."

He nodded. He had grown up around such things. "I was a happy adolescent," he confided.

She blinked, then her eyes grew wide. "You... You..."

"I learned how to massage sore tigress muscles when I was twelve. By thirteen..."

"You must have had sex with...with...like everyone here! Oh, my—"

"Not sex," he explained quickly. "A tigress does not allow a dragon to sport in their cave."

She frowned. "Then what exactly did you do with them?"

He shrugged. "I massaged them. I stimulated them. And I learned the ways of control."

"But you said you were a *happy* adolescent."

He grinned. "I did not always act in control. And a tigress must practice tongue technique on someone. I was all too willing—"

She held up her hand. "I got it! I got it! Wow, you must have had some childhood."

It took him a moment to realize she didn't understand. "I was surrounded by tigresses, Tracy. I could experience carnal delights known to few men, much less teenagers. But…" He shook his head. "But today when I was signing contracts, when I ate my lunch, even when I was deep in negotiations with Stephen, all I could think of was this moment tonight when I would come see you."

"Me?" She raised her eyes doubtfully. "Because you want…" Her eyes canted downward to the bed.

He almost laughed. If the idea weren't so very tempting, he would have. "Endless sex grew wearisome to me as an adolescent. Now…" He shrugged. "I want… I want to hear how your studies progress," he lied.

She snorted in disbelief. "Yeah, right."

He grimaced, frustrated with his inability to express himself. "At the end of my day, my spirit quiets, and I think of you. I want to be with you. I want…" He sighed. "I gain strength from you, and I don't even know why."

She stared at him. His words seemed to have thrown her into as much confusion as he felt. He knew better than to bare his soul to a tigress, and yet here he was, making the same mistake again. He shifted to leave. Her silence was too unbearable. He did not want to hear that she had chosen Stephen over him, that—

"I understand the joy of family responsibility," she said. "But one thing doesn't fit. One piece of the Nathan Gao puzzle isn't complete yet. Why the United States? I'll bet you could have gone to school here in Hong Kong. Why go all the way to Illinois?"

He blinked, thrown by her words. And yet, hadn't she said back in the United States that the only reason she was coming here was to find out about his past? Could that be true? Could she really have come all the way here just to learn about him?

Apparently so, because she was probing in places he didn't truly want her to go. So he turned back to her with a benign smile. "The United States has excellent schools, and Illinois is the best for business."

She waved the thought away. "Yeah, yeah. I've heard that before. But you sacrificed a lot to get to the United States. Schooling is great, but there's another reason."

He looked down at her, knowing that she would not stop pushing unless he did something drastic. So he crossed to her side, using this as an excuse to touch her, to caress her, to give in to what he had wanted to do for so long.

"There is no hidden motive, Tracy. I chose a school and put everything I had into getting there." He touched her face. Just a soft caress on her cheek, but she closed her eyes and moved into his hand to better appreciate his touch. This was not a tigress movement. It was something Tracy did whenever he touched her, whenever he was near her. She appreciated the moment and loved his caress. And for that he adored her even more.

But her mind did not stop probing. "Were you running from something, Nathan? What could be so awful that you would leave your siblings, abandon the temple, and go halfway around the world to escape?"

He didn't answer. Instead, he leaned in to kiss her shoulder.

"I'm not letting go of this, Nathan. You can't distract me," she said. But even as she spoke, he felt the tremor that went through her body as he feathered his lips across her neck.

"There is no secret, Tracy. I fell in love. I have already told you this." He pushed at the blanket, nudging with his lips and teeth so that the sheet fell away to expose her breasts.

"Nathan…" she whispered, the word half plea, half protest.

He smiled as he crossed the tiny distance to her breast. He liked that he could make her tremble, could make her voice soft and breathy. And he loved when she grabbed his shoulders, clenching tighter as he clasped her nipple in his teeth.

Then she caught his face. Her fingers were strong against his cheeks as she lifted him to her mouth. He went willingly, claiming her mouth with his, thrusting inside her, drawing those gasping sounds of delight from between her lips.

But then she broke away, her hands still holding his head. He could have stepped away. He could have fought her hold, but she looked him in the eyes. She did not glance coyly away; she did not try to seduce with a flutter of lashes or a sly wink. She opened her round eyes even rounder, and she asked one last time, "Why did you go so far away from your home?"

"I told you," he answered honestly. "I fell in love."

She nodded as if expecting that answer. "With the redhead?"

"With all of them. But yes, she was the latest." He sat back on a sigh, his hands trailing across her body, stroking idly down her neck, across her shoulder, fondling her breast. Her skin was so white, her body so familiar in some ways, and yet so different in others. "Tigresses use sex. They learn from it, they experience it, they take and create energy from it."

"But they don't fall in love, do they?" she asked.

"No. They don't."

Tracy exhaled on a huff. "Sounds like a rather selfish

religion to me. I mean, what's the point of sex without love? At least affection. Something."

"Immortality," he answered. He lifted his gaze from where he stroked across her belly before teasing into the lower curls. "You have been to the Chamber of a Thousand Swinging Lanterns. You know better than I do what a tigress seeks."

"So you loved her and she used you to gain heaven." Her voice was tight with anger. "They all used you. Every single one of them beginning with your mother, using you without regard to what you felt or wanted."

He nodded, unable to lie to her. "I can lose myself in love," he said. "And I could not stop from loving them. The smallest piece of affection, the slightest kindness, and I was lost."

"Oh, Nathan…" she murmured.

"So I left—as far away as possible—and I swore I would never come back. I would never, ever see them again." His simple words could not possibly communicate his anger, his frustration and his pain. And yet, she understood.

"I'm so sorry," she breathed. "And now you're back here because of me. Because you think I belong here. With them."

He shrugged. "I came to sell the temple. And I brought a great new tigress with me." Then he took her hands and spoke as honestly as he could. "I cannot blame them for choosing heaven over me."

"I can," she said. "I blame them with every breath I take."

He saw the honesty in her eyes. He saw her fierce anger because other women had discarded him. Because his mother often forgot him, no matter what he did for her. Because of all the tiny slights delivered by tigresses to their men of the moment. She saw them, and she burned with hot anger for him. And in that second, he knew why she brought him strength.

He loved her.

She was the well of goodness that he had searched for all his life. She gave openly and honestly, and for that he would adore her forever.

"Let me help you," he whispered. "One last time, let me help you with your studies. Let me give you all my energy, all my strength, all that I have. Let—"

Tracy cut off his words with a kiss. She surged upward, invading his mouth with her own power and fierce beauty. "We're doing this together, Nathan." She threw off the blanket and immediately reached for his shirt, unbuttoning it with quick movements. He grabbed her hands in instinctive reaction, but all too quickly his grip softened into a caress.

"I do not need to be undressed for—"

"Pish posh. I say you do." She smiled. "And I'm the tigress, aren't I?"

He almost laughed. "You are like no tigress I know."

"Good."

"You are the best of them. Even untrained, you are better than all of them." Then he kissed her. He stroked her lips. He tasted her sweetness. And when he pulled back, she blinked in dazed delight. He loved that even now his kisses could make her eyes go hazy. Then he looked down as she tugged at the fastening of his pants. "I am only a man, Tracy. Do not tempt me too far."

"Yadda yadda. I want you naked." She pushed down his boxers and gripped him. Her handling was inexpert, but her touch was like fire.

"Tracy!" he gasped. "You have to remain a virgin." He managed a firm grip on her wrists, but he could not keep her fingers quiet. "Tracy—don't!"

She stilled, and he exhaled a stuttering breath. She leaned in, and this time she was the one stroking across his lips, nipping at his mouth and thrusting herself inside him. "I've come to a decision of my own, Nathan. And guess what? You're part of it."

# 19

EVEN AFTER THREE DAYS at the temple and even more with Nathan, Tracy had little understanding of what a tigress was or what she was supposed to do. At the moment, none of it mattered. She knew Nathan. She understood the forces that drove him, and she loved him all the better for it. They were alike in that—both giving all they could for their families while still trying to eke out a place for themselves. And they were alike in this, as well—this fierce passion that sparked whenever they touched.

"Tigresses do not go to heaven together," he said as she pulled his shirt off. "The journey is always alone."

"Doesn't sound like much of a journey," she answered.

He paused, the chiseled angles of his face smoothing as he touched her cheek. "You can never be successful at the temple with that attitude, Tracy."

She thought about that, about the beauty of the women in this place, the exquisite sensuality of their every moment, and most of all that wonderful place he called *heaven*. She brought all those to mind and then threw them away.

"Then I guess I don't want to be a tigress." There. She'd said it aloud, and the decision felt right. "I want you." She kissed him again. She put her heart in her touch, her soul in her caress, and she felt him shudder against her lips.

"You don't know what you're saying," he protested weakly. "You don't realize—"

"When are you going to accept that I can make up my own mind?"

She waited silently for his answer. He was absolutely still, his eyes piercingly direct despite the shadows. She could see the shock there and the gratitude. That cut at her the most. He was grateful that someone would choose him when he was the most amazing, giving man she had ever met.

His smile came slowly, but oh so sexily. "I believe I am done being noble." His hands found her breasts in a feathery brush that was light, reverent, and set her entire chest tingling. Then he kissed her left breast and lightning zinged from his mouth into her, all the way through to her toes.

He suckled gently and she felt the pull of energy. The tingles in her chest concentrated tighter as he tongued her nipple. Then he raised up and blew a gentle whisper across her. The flash of cold made her back arch in sensation. "Open for me," he whispered.

"Always. Forever." They were the only words she could speak, and his eyes darkened with yearning.

The sight touched her so deeply that nothing else was needed. The energy floodgates opened, pouring into him like a brilliant river.

"No…" he cried, though his back arched and his thighs tensed. "This. Is. For you."

"For us," she gasped. Then she tightened her thighs around him. She could do no more than rub her legs against his pants, whimpering at the cloth. "Take them off," she ordered.

"Harness your energy," he said. "Ride the chi to heaven." Tracy almost growled at him. He didn't understand!

None of that stuff made sense to her. Nathan made sense. Nathan drew her. So she focused on him, directing her energy at him. And as she thought of him, her heart swelled with love. She had no clue exactly when she had fallen for him, but the love was there now, pulsing with joy. And so she gave him that, too, and her love multiplied the energy river a hundredfold. "Nathan," she whispered, trying to find the words to voice her discovery.

Her thoughts stuttered to an abrupt halt as his hand slid down her belly and into her folds. His fingers were expert at touching her, at circling and stroking. He slid into her while his thumb burrowed upward. She felt it—thick and hard. She was so sensitized to his touch that she could feel the texture of his thumbprint as it rolled over her clit.

Her belly was quivering, her entire body alive with power. It would take very little to begin the rest: the contraction of orgasm, the ecstasy of seeming flight, the joy that took her to heaven. He had done this once before for her, but not this time. Not like this.

She jerked backward from him, grabbing his shoulders with all the strength she could muster. Then she toppled him over and ripped his pants away before quickly mounting into position. "You," she gasped. "I want you!" She knew where he was, arrow straight and as hard as steel. His shoulders where she gripped him were like iron, and she dug her nails in.

"We can't, Tracy! You will lose immortality!" His words were tight as he fought himself.

"I know. I want you," she answered. "I love you." Then she bore down onto him as hard as she could, feeling herself widen and open. Something inside snapped and a flash of pain cut through her consciousness. But the sensation only added to her power. She poured the pain into her river of energy and the light seemed to grow brighter, the fire hotter. She tightened her legs, loving the feel of him thick and hard inside her. So full. So deep.

"Tracy…" he whispered. Then his voice grew richer, darker. "Tracy." His eyes blackened and his nostrils flared.

He began to move. Slowly at first. Withdrawing while she arched, as if he dragged some central part of her with him when he pulled back. He swallowed, and she watched the ripple of his throat muscles, but all too soon her gaze slid back up to his eyes.

He thrust inside her, and she gasped. But as he withdrew, something deep inside her went with him. Her energy or power. She didn't know. But it followed his movements—stretching out as he withdrew then compressing tight as he returned.

"Nathan…" she breathed. "Something…"

"My yang," he said. He did it again. "As you gave me your yin, I return to you my yang."

She didn't understand, but that didn't matter. This wasn't something for her mind to understand. He withdrew again, pulling the power with him. And when he thrust, her energies increased. Orgasm hit—a wave of pleasure, expanding through her body. But that wasn't the end.

While she cried out, he continued to withdraw and thrust, the piston of energy intensifying her orgasm. Each contraction felt deeper, harder and more amazing than the last. And still he continued.

"Nathan!" she cried, not having any other word than that. His name, his yang, his power. He thrust again, and lightning surged up her spine, throwing her head back and angling her hips for even deeper penetration. Then he slammed into her one last time.

"Tracy!" His bellow was the smallest echo of the explosion that roared through her body. He climaxed, and his yang roared through her system. Jet fuel set alight!

And they flew.

STARS PULSED ALL around her. No, they hummed. They danced. Like rich earth and bright sun, all was love and harmony and beauty. Tracy lifted her arms to the music and laughed in sheer delight.

She was in heaven again. The Chamber of a Thousand Swinging Lanterns where she was surrounded by light and sounds, colors of every texture, and joy that permeated into a sense of total love. It was everything she remembered and so much more that she had forgotten. She was standing in total love, but it had no direction. And as fantastical as it was, she wanted more. She wanted a focus, a single love. She wanted Nathan.

"I am here."

She spun around, giggling in delight when she saw him beside her. He stood in a raiment of white light, and she knew without understanding that she saw his spirit. She saw his love for his family, his fears for the future; she saw all that she already knew. And she loved him yet more.

She wrapped her arms around him. "I am so glad you are here!"

"You brought me," he whispered as he gazed about in awe.

*You brought yourselves.* The sound came from everywhere, and yet the vibration of it seemed to be right inside her—warm and loving.

Nathan must have heard it—felt it?—as well because he dropped to his knees, his forehead pressed to the ground in a kowtow. Tracy bent in an awkward curtsy. There wasn't a person or even a direction to curtsy to, and yet the feeling inside her seemed to smile in welcome. It was like a warm caress to her heart that held a whisper of eternity.

*All of heaven delights with you!* The darkness around them seemed to shimmer with music. Tracy thought she saw people or structures, but they weren't shapes so much as thoughts and joyous feelings given form. Except the forms went by so fast and were so complicated that her mind couldn't grasp them. They were beautiful. All was beautiful, and Tracy's whole being tingled brightly in echo.

"How is this possible?" Nathan breathed, awe and shock rippling through the light that was him.

Heaven laughed in such a bubbling vibration that Tracy giggled. *All things are possible here. All things are possible there, too.*

"Where?" Tracy asked though she already knew the answer.

*Wherever you are. Heaven is within you. It always has been.* A light sparkled across her in a kiss suffused with love. *We will see you again!*

They fell. Hand in hand, they tumbled backward. Both immediately surged upward, trying desperately to remain, but they kept their hands linked. Buoying each other, they hovered a moment longer. "When?" they cried in unison. "When can we come back?"

*Whenever you like,* was the echoing answer.

They lost their lightness. Tracy's being became heavy

and slow. And the more she struggled, the heavier she became. Within seconds, her spirit tumbled back into her body. Her last conscious sensation was Nathan's hand squeezing her own.

# 20

TRACY WOKE SLOWLY, her body heavy and cold. There was movement beside her—in her—and she opened her eyes.

Nathan. He was sliding sideways, and for a moment, she could still see the glowing beauty of his heavenly soul. He was so beautiful that it brought tears to her eyes. But then she blinked, and when she opened her eyes again, the glow was gone. And yet, he was still wonderful. She didn't need heavenly vision to know that.

"I love you," she whispered.

He didn't answer as he collapsed beside her on the bed with a muffled grunt. She might have smiled at that, except she abruptly realized she was already grinning. "We went to heaven. Together."

"Lummmmph," he said, his face buried in the pillow. "Mmm unnn lummmph."

She had no idea what he was saying, but she felt too heavy to ask. That was the only drawback to coming back to earth: the heaviness, the cold. The loneliness.

She made a Herculean effort and rolled onto her side to press a kiss against Nathan's face. She wanted to talk. Had he seen what she had? Did he remember the light? The beauty? Instead, totally different words came out.

"I love you," she repeated.

He rolled onto his side so that he faced her. He looked so relaxed, so happy. "So much love," he murmured. "For you."

He reached out to touch her. She thought he might stroke her face, but his gesture was clumsy. He was probably feeling as heavy as she was. His hand fell to her side and he tugged. He was pulling her closer to him.

It was exactly what she wanted, too, so she curled her body into his heat. She closed her eyes only when she could hear the steady thump of his heart. His hand curved about her back, tightening as he drew her even closer.

They slept.

She woke hours later to an empty bed but a not-so-empty bedroom. Tracy blinked, working to focus her eyes. Her hand extended to where Nathan had been. Empty. And her eyes focused on a person sitting across from her: the Tigress Mother. The woman sat primly in a chair, her eyes piercing with a cold anger.

"Choose, cub. Heaven or earth?"

Tracy blinked, her vision clearing enough to realize that the sun was high in the sky. It was well into day. Had Nathan left? Was he already flying back to the U.S.? The thought had her pushing upright in bed, fear tightening her chest.

"Choose," the Tigress Mother repeated. "I will not waste time on a girl who wishes to remain ignorant."

Tracy closed her eyes a moment and inhaled deeply. She smelled Nathan on her sheets, and she remembered so much—and too little—of what had happened. The memories were beginning to fade, but she still retained the most important part.

"Do you know what I learned in heaven?" she asked as she pushed the covers off.

"What did you learn?" Her tone was sharp as she leaned forward.

Tracy grinned. "That it is possible to have it all—heaven and earth. Together." Then she climbed out of bed and began to pack.

THE FLIGHT HOME WASN'T nearly as exciting as the flight out. On the way to China, she'd been excited to visit a new country, couldn't wait to see the tigress temple, and of course Nathan had been her perfect companion. The trip home had only herself, Mr. Ruhleder, her snoring companion in seat 4A and a gnawing question: Why had Nathan left? Without a word, without so much as a kiss goodbye, he had gone on his early morning flight while she had slept in blissful ignorance. By the time she made it back to Champaign, she was either going to kiss him soundly or kick him in the balls. Maybe both.

She landed to bright skies and blustery winds. Just the kind of November day that usually had her outside with her face to the wind while thinking of the hot cider she ought to get but never did. Today, the wind blew her straight to a cab, which she directed to the apartment building.

She pulled out her cell phone and cursed it. Without electricity at the temple, she'd had no way to charge the damn thing, so it was completely useless. She tossed it back into her purse and glared at the scenery. Then—for the zillionth time—she tried to remember her last night with Nathan. She'd said the words. She'd said, "I love you," at least once, maybe more.

But had he? Had he said he loved her? She didn't think

so. She had felt loved. She had felt a lot of things. But was his kind of love the same thing as her kind of love? Was he really being noble and letting her choose her own path without pressure from him? Or was he just ducking out to avoid an ugly scene? Was he…? Did he…? For eight thousand miles she'd been asking the same questions. And now…

The cab pulled around the corner and had to slow down to a near crawl. She looked out the window and gasped. She counted three squad cars and…Joey? Was that Joey standing in front of the apartment building?

Her stomach dropped. She'd completely forgotten Detective Mike McKay. He couldn't be arresting Nathan, could he? Oh, crap!

She dug into her purse, grabbing bills—both U.S. and Chinese—to throw at the cabbie. "Get as close as you can," she said, her heart beating painfully in her throat. "Oh, hell."

Joey was standing to one side, just watching the action. But there was no action! There were no signs of the policemen, only the black-and-whites and Mike's blue Buick. She dove out of the cab the moment it stopped and ran straight for her brother. "Joey!"

Her turned around, using his hand to shield his eyes. "Sis? Wow!"

"What's going on? Why are the cops here?"

"Mike called me. Said he had to make an arrest. Something about a crime ring—"

"It's not true!" Tracy cried, then turned and headed for the building only to be tackled by her brother.

"Whoa! Sis!" Her face hit the dirt with an *umpth!* "You can't go up there. They're arresting him."

"Let me go!" She pushed at him, but Joey was line-backer strong.

"You can't interfere!" her brother said from on top of her. "They've got guns. Ow!"

Her squirming had no effect. All 183 pounds of her brother were keeping her flat, no matter how much she kicked. "Joey, you're crushing me," Tracy lied. If she couldn't push him off, maybe she could trick him into releasing her.

It worked! Her brother's weight immediately eased, but it wasn't enough to release her legs.

"Damn it, Trace—stay still!" her brother huffed. "This is serious! There's a drug runner in there!"

"There is not!" she retorted out of reflex. Then she frowned. Drug runner?

*Bam! Bam! Bam!*

The sound of gunshots electrified Tracy. Joey looked up, which gave her the opportunity to shove for all she was worth. Her brother was thrown off balance and Tracy scrambled out from underneath him. Then she was running, her mind filled with images of Nathan shot and bleeding to death, while Joey bellowed behind her.

"Tracy!"

He wasn't as fast as she was. She flew up the stairs, her breath lost to gasps and sobs. Nathan couldn't be dead. Not before she'd had a chance to kick him in the balls. Not before—

Someone tackled her from the side. She landed hard against the wall, and her head bounced painfully. A moment later, she was flat on the second-floor landing while a behemoth sat on her chest. A behemoth who smelled really, really familiar.

She blinked and tried to draw breath. It took forever for her eyes to focus, but when they did she saw exactly what she was looking for: Nathan, whole and healthy. And smiling. It was a slow smile at first, but it grew quickly, spreading from his lips to his eyes, all the way through his entire body. She had no idea how she knew his body was grinning, but it was. Or maybe she was the one suffused with happiness. He was here. They were finally together.

"Nathan," she breathed.

"You're here," he whispered from on top of her. His chest was covering hers; his arms were shielding her face, and most important, his head was tucked so close to hers.

"They can't arrest you," she gasped. "You haven't done anything wrong."

Then Mike's stern voice broke in, rough with irritation. "What the hell are you doing running into a fire-fight, Tracy?"

Nathan started to lift off her, but Tracy held him tightly. She wasn't letting him go until she decided what she was going to do with him. "I'm sorry, Detective McKay, but Mr. Gao is innocent. He hasn't done anything wrong. I'd swear to that in a court of law." She looked over Nathan's shoulder at her friend, who was busy holstering his gun.

Mike blinked at her. "Have you hit your head?"

She shook her head. "I'm fine, but Nathan—Mr. Gao—"

"Has been really helpful. I heard something that day we were fixing Mr. Gao's sink. So, after I cleared Nathan Gao of any illegal activity himself, I asked if we could use his apartment to stake out his neighbor." He gestured behind himself. Tracy had to lift her head a little higher to see the tenant of 4B—Mr. Loud TV who was always on his phone to his bookie—being led out of his apartment in handcuffs. Mike shook his head. "Easy story—gambling debts, foray into drug running, stupidity all around." Then he looked back at Tracy. "Didn't you get my messages?"

"You're arresting 4B?" she asked, her mind finally catching up to reality. Meanwhile, Nathan hadn't stopped looking at her.

"You're here," he murmured, his eyes sparkling. "You came back."

"You need to get up now, Tracy," Mike said. "We've got to bring the felon down the stairs."

It took Tracy a moment to realize she had Nathan in a death grip and that they were lying together in the middle of the stairway landing. It took a moment longer for her to coax her hands into releasing him. Once he was free, he stood up easily, gently bringing her up right beside him. And then he arched one of those too-sexy eyebrows at her before leaning down to brush some of the mud off her crumpled blouse.

"Yeah, yeah," she said as she batted away his hands. "My brother only tackles people in the mud. And I'm still thinking about kick—"

"Tracy!" Mike interrupted again. "The felon?" He gestured to handcuffed 4B, who glared at everyone. Behind him stood three more cops, all waiting to climb down the stairs.

"Right," said Tracy as she and Nathan filed down and out of the building. Joey was waiting by the front door. Apparently there had been a cop stationed down there. Tracy had managed to surprise him, flying right past, but Joey had been caught and held.

Then came a long hour of chaos and interruptions. 4B was whisked away immediately, but Tracy still had to give a statement both as a sort-of witness and the owner of the building. That didn't take long, but answering questions from tenants and neighbors and media—well, that took longer. And how mortifying that was, to stand in a muddy blouse before news cameras. And all the while, she kept one hand gripped firmly on Nathan's arm. She wasn't letting go for anything! But at least she'd decided not to kick him on TV.

Then finally, miraculously, it was all done. The tenants were convinced all was safe. Better yet—from their perspective at least—Tracy had decided to delay selling the building. A drug bust on television was too damaging to the price. Joey naturally leaped on that thought, still hoping to take a year off to manage the building. She hadn't argued—yet—and so he'd immediately disappeared to inspect the damage left by 4B. Apparently, the man had really bad aim. All three bullets had hit his television. He wasn't dead because even with a weapon, he hadn't seemed scary enough for the cops to shoot him.

That left Tracy and Nathan alone in his apartment. Nathan was making tea…of course. And Tracy was left just standing there, staring at his gorgeous body and thinking what she would have done if he'd been shot. The pain from merely the idea was unbearable.

To hell with subtlety, she decided. She'd waited too long not to be blunt. "Why'd you leave?" she demanded.

"I woke and found your mother in my room."

She wasn't sure he could hear her. He was busy pouring hot water into two mugs. But then he walked over and pressed a mug into her hands. "I left because I had to. They couldn't find me in your room in the morning. It would have…"

"What? What would have happened?"

"It would have been bad for you."

She felt her hands clench around the steaming mug. But rather than throw it in his face, she carefully set it down. "Might have been bad? Bad was waking up to your mother, not you. Bad was having to fly home alone wondering the whole time. Bad was—"

"Wondering what?"

She blinked, her tirade interrupted. "What?"

"What were you wondering?"

Now she did throw up her hands. "I told you I loved you! I gave up immortality for you! Or at least I thought I did. I…I love you, damn it! And you were gone!"

He swallowed and set his own mug down. She was close enough to feel his heat, and yet he didn't touch her. He seemed uncertain and apologetic all at the same time.

"Nathan! Talk to me! Or I swear I'm going to kick you in—"

"We went to heaven, and I saw…" His eyes grew hazy. "I understand now. I know why the tigresses search so hard for it. It was…" He shook his head. "It was more than I ever thought or believed."

She stared at him. "I know. But I gave that up…" She swallowed. "You thought I'd change my mind, didn't you? After going there with me, you knew what it was like. You knew and thought I'd be like all the rest." She abruptly made a fist and slammed him hard in the shoulder. "Damn it! Haven't you figured out by now that I'm not like all the rest? I'm not going to dump you for any *place*—even a heavenly one. I—*umph*."

He was kissing her. He was burying himself in her, and as angry and frustrated as she was, Tracy couldn't hold him off. She wanted to touch him as much as he seemed to need her. But eventually, she was able to pull back.

"Nathan—"

"I had to go," he said. "By contract. Stephen made me put it in the contract that I would leave the very next morning." He shrugged. "I think he wanted to make another play for you with me gone."

She thought back. Stephen had been there that afternoon, but her decision had already been made. She'd refused to see the man, sent a message that their partnership was off, then got Nathan's brother to bicycle-cart her to the airport.

"But I didn't leave right away," Nathan continued as he pulled something out of his pocket. "I stopped long enough to buy something. Because I thought… I hoped…" He dropped down onto one knee and held up a ring box from an exclusive Hong Kong jeweler.

Tracy stared at it. Then she looked at him, her thoughts whirling.

"I have enough money now," he said. "To pay for my schooling. For yours. For whatever stockbrokers need to—"

"I don't care about that," she whispered. "I don't care about the money. If I did, I would have stayed with Stephen."

"Will you marry me, Tracy? I love you. I lied when I said I love all my students. What I feel for you goes way beyond anything I've ever done or felt." His hands were shaking but his eyes were crystal clear and filled with hope. "It's love like I can't describe. I want to go to bed with you every night, work my fingers to the bone for our children during the day, and then—"

This time she was the one who cut him off with kisses. She wrapped her arms around him and didn't give either of them time to breathe. Not for a long, long time. When she finally broke away from him, she whispered, "Yes. Yesyesyesyesyesyesyes!" Then she dropped her forehead against his, her heartbeat still skittering inside her chest. "So, wanna take me to heaven for our honeymoon?"

Nathan lifted his head, and the look in his eyes took her breath away. "Anywhere, anytime, anyplace. Tracy, so long as you are by my side, I will go wherever you want."

She smiled, stunned to realize that she felt as much love now as she ever had in heaven. She was surrounded, infused and steeped in love. And it was all for him and from him. "We're already there, aren't we?" she whispered in awe. "We're already in heaven."

"Yes," he answered. Then he kissed her and she realized that it was true. Everything they needed was within them. And what was within them was love.

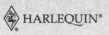

# REQUEST YOUR FREE BOOKS!

## 2 FREE NOVELS PLUS 2 FREE GIFTS!

HARLEQUIN®

*Blaze*®

**Red-hot reads!**

**YES!** Please send me 2 FREE Harlequin® Blaze® novels and my 2 FREE gifts. After receiving them, if I don't wish to receive any more books, I can return the shipping statement marked "cancel." If I don't cancel, I will receive 6 brand-new novels every month and be billed just $3.99 per book in the U.S., or $4.47 per book in Canada, plus 25¢ shipping and handling per book and applicable taxes, if any*. That's a savings of at least 15% off the cover price! I understand that accepting the 2 free books and gifts places me under no obligation to buy anything. I can always return a shipment and cancel at any time. Even if I never buy another book from Harlequin, the two free books and gifts are mine to keep forever.

151 HDN EF3W   351 HDN EF3X

| | |
|---|---|
| Name | (PLEASE PRINT) |
| Address | Apt. |
| City | State/Prov. Zip/Postal Code |

Signature (if under 18, a parent or guardian must sign)

Mail to the **Harlequin Reader Service**®:
**IN U.S.A.:** P.O. Box 1867, Buffalo, NY 14240-1867
**IN CANADA:** P.O. Box 609, Fort Erie, Ontario L2A 5X3

Not valid to current Harlequin Blaze subscribers.

**Want to try two free books from another line?**
**Call 1-800-873-8635 or visit www.morefreebooks.com.**

\* Terms and prices subject to change without notice. NY residents add applicable sales tax. Canadian residents will be charged applicable provincial taxes and GST. This offer is limited to one order per household. All orders subject to approval. Credit or debit balances in a customer's account(s) may be offset by any other outstanding balance owed by or to the customer. Please allow 4 to 6 weeks for delivery.

**Your Privacy:** Harlequin is committed to protecting your privacy. Our Privacy Policy is available online at www.eHarlequin.com or upon request from the Reader Service. From time to time we make our lists of customers available to reputable firms who may have a product or service of interest to you. If you would prefer we not share your name and address, please check here. ☐

HB07

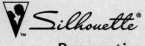

## Romantic
# SUSPENSE

*Sparked by Danger,*
*Fueled by Passion.*

When Tech Sergeant Jacob "Mako" Stone opens
his door to a mysterious woman without a past,
he knows his time off is over. As threats to Dee's
life bring her and Jacob together, she must set
aside her pride and accept the help of the military
hero with too many secrets of his own.

# *Out of Uniform*
# by Catherine Mann

*Available February wherever you buy books.*

# Texas Hold 'Em

### When it comes to love, the stakes are high

Sixteen years ago, Luke Chisum dated
Becky Parker on a dare…before going
on to break her heart. Now the former
River Bluff daredevil is back, rekindling
desire and tempting Becky to pick up
where they left off. But this time she has
to resist or Luke could discover the secret
she's kept locked away all these years.…

*Look for*

# TEXAS BLUFF

## *by Linda Warren*

### #1470

*Available February 2008
wherever you buy books.*

HSR71470